Saika Kuozaki
The world's most powerful mage and headmistress of the mage-training institute Void's Garden.

Kuroe Karasuma
Saika's attendant. Carefully guarding a major secret.

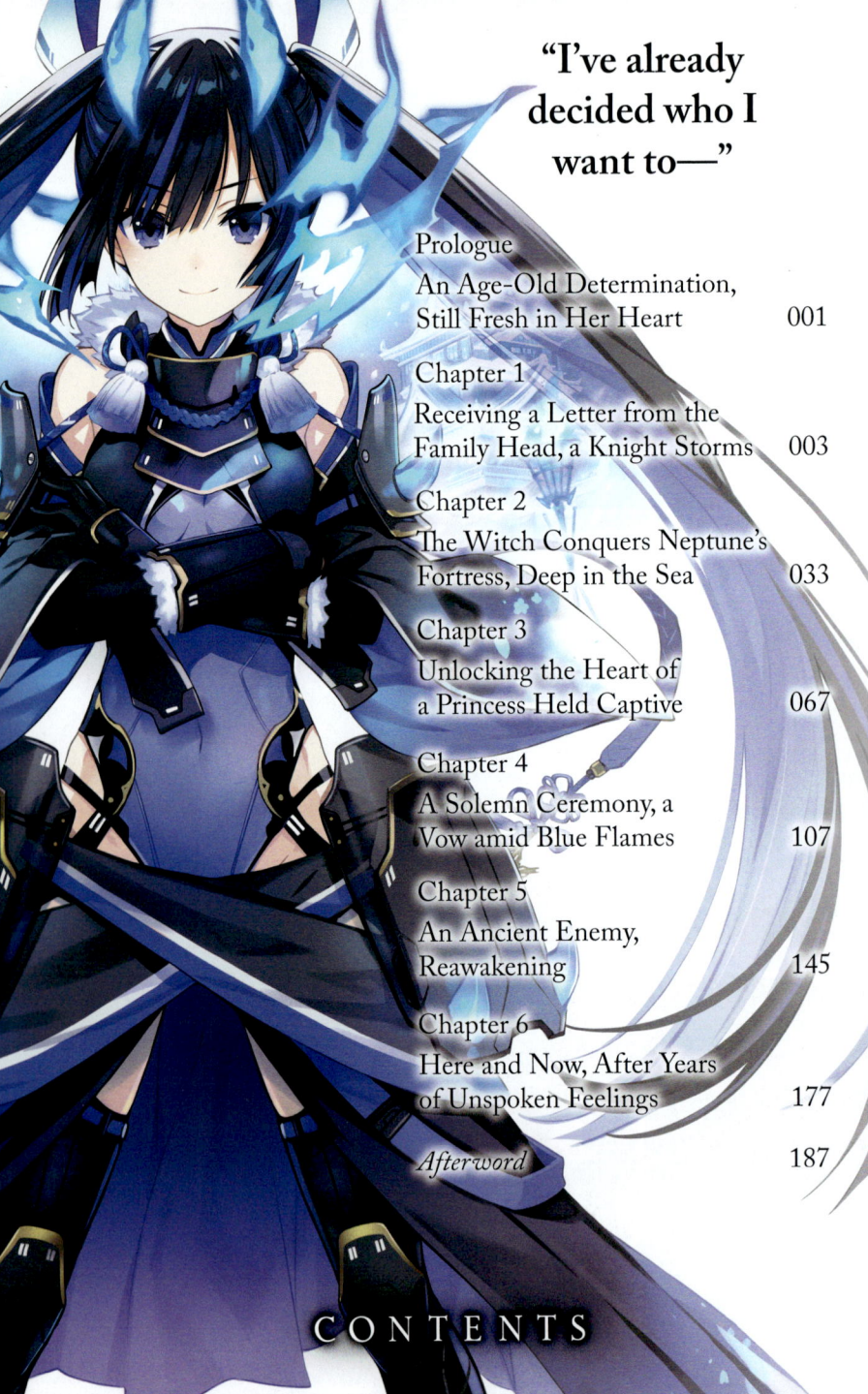

> "I've already decided who I want to—"

Prologue
An Age-Old Determination,
Still Fresh in Her Heart — 001

Chapter 1
Receiving a Letter from the
Family Head, a Knight Storms — 003

Chapter 2
The Witch Conquers Neptune's
Fortress, Deep in the Sea — 033

Chapter 3
Unlocking the Heart of
a Princess Held Captive — 067

Chapter 4
A Solemn Ceremony, a
Vow amid Blue Flames — 107

Chapter 5
An Ancient Enemy,
Reawakening — 145

Chapter 6
Here and Now, After Years
of Unspoken Feelings — 177

Afterword — 187

CONTENTS

KING'S PROPOSAL

Volume 3

◆ The Lapis Knight ◆

Koushi Tachibana

Illustration by **Tsunako**

NEW YORK

Vol. 3

Koushi Tachibana

Translation by Haydn Trowell
Cover art by Tsunako

This book is a work of fiction. Names, characters, places, and incidents are the product of the author's imagination or are used fictitiously. Any resemblance to actual events, locales, or persons, living or dead, is coincidental.

OSAMA NO PROPOSAL Vol. 3 RURI NO KISHI
©Koushi Tachibana, Tsunako 2022
First published in Japan in 2022 by KADOKAWA CORPORATION, Tokyo.
English translation rights arranged with KADOKAWA CORPORATION, Tokyo, through TUTTLE-MORI AGENCY, INC., Tokyo.

English translation © 2023 by Yen Press, LLC

Yen Press, LLC supports the right to free expression and the value of copyright. The purpose of copyright is to encourage writers and artists to produce the creative works that enrich our culture.

The scanning, uploading, and distribution of this book without permission is a theft of the author's intellectual property. If you would like permission to use material from the book (other than for review purposes), please contact the publisher. Thank you for your support of the author's rights.

Yen On
150 West 30th Street, 19th Floor
New York, NY 10001

Visit us at yenpress.com
facebook.com/yenpress
twitter.com/yenpress
yenpress.tumblr.com
instagram.com/yenpress

First Yen On Edition: September 2023
Edited by Yen On Editorial: Shella Wu
Designed by Yen Press Design: Madelaine Norman, Wendy Chan

Yen On is an imprint of Yen Press, LLC.
The Yen On name and logo are trademarks of Yen Press, LLC.

The publisher is not responsible for websites (or their content) that are not owned by the publisher.

Library of Congress Cataloging-in-Publication Data
Names: Tachibana, Koushi, 1986- author. | Tsunako, illustrator. | Trowell, Haydn, translator.
Title: King's proposal / Koushi Tachibana ; illustration by Tsunako ; translation by Haydn Trowell.
Other titles: Osama no proposal. English
Description: First Yen On edition. | New York, NY : Yen On, 2022- |
Identifiers: LCCN 2022027184 | ISBN 9781975351502 (v. 1 ; trade paperback) |
  ISBN 9781975351632 (v. 2 ; trade paperback) | ISBN 9781975370039 (v. 3 ; trade paperback)
Subjects: CYAC: Fantasy. | Witches—Fiction. | Magic—Fiction. | Schools—Fiction. |
  Identity—Fiction. | LCGFT: Fantasy fiction. | Witch fiction. | School fiction. | Light novels.
Classification: LCC PZ7.1.T296 Kin 2022 | DDC [Fic]—dc23
LC record available at https://lccn.loc.gov/2022027184

ISBNs: 978-1-9753-7003-9 (paperback)
       978-1-9753-7004-6 (ebook)

10 9 8 7 6 5 4 3 2 1

LSC-C

Printed in the United States of America

KING'S PROPOSAL

The Lapis Knight

In sickness and in pain.

In sorrow and in grief.

In poverty and in despair.

My brother has always been there for me.

So this time, I'll be the one to protect him.

Prologue
An Age-Old Determination, ⇠ Still Fresh in Her Heart ⇢

Life is a series of choices, and time is irreversible.

If there was ever a single moment that had defined Ruri Fuyajoh's life, it could only have been that day.

That day—seven years ago. The young Ruri had been seated before the head of the Fuyajoh clan in the family mansion.

She was surrounded by a group of masked girls, and her mother was behind her.

It was such a strange space. Yet Ruri neither felt uneasy nor found it to be in any way out of the ordinary. She merely focused on looking straight ahead toward the far end of the room.

Why? Because the flame of determination had been kindled inside her.

"Do you mean it?" a quiet voice echoed from behind a bamboo blind that shielded the elevated platform at the end of the room.

"...Yes," Ruri answered calmly as she held her gaze firm. "I will become a mage—strong enough to beat anyone. A mage with the power to defeat any annihilation factor."

At this declaration, the girls seated around her began to giggle.

Well, that response wasn't entirely unreasonable. After all, this was coming from someone who couldn't even manifest her first substantiation. The girls' reaction was entirely natural.

"Quiet."

But the voice sounding from behind the bamboo blind quickly silenced them.

"Ruri. A mage's power lies in the strength of their heart... Are you truly prepared?"

"Yes," she answered without the slightest hesitation. "So long as enemies seek to ravage the world, I will defeat them... I'll be as strong as I need to be. So please..." She paused, clenching her fists tightly. "Please let my brother live a normal life."

Chapter 1
Receiving a Letter from the Family Head, a Knight Storms

The world was dyed in five colors.

Mushiki Kuga gazed at the fantastic scene spread out before him from his vantage point on the edge of a towering skyscraper in the void.

It was such a strange view. The space, so vast that you couldn't tell where it ended, was divided into five sections like a cake into slices, each characterized by wholly unique scenery. It was as if he had cut up several postcards and glued them back together as his mood fancied.

It was hard to believe that it was all real. In fact, if the old Mushiki had seen this, he would have thought it was a dream or an illusion.

But perhaps that was only to be expected.

After all, gathered here now—

—were the mages lauded as the best in the whole world.

"Allow me to provide an overview of the incident once again," a clear voice echoed throughout that five-colored world.

Curiously, the voice seemed to fill every corner of that vast, endless space.

"Clara Tokishima, a mage belonging to Shadow Tower, led a cohort of her followers to stage an uprising during the exhibition match held the other day at Void's Garden… Her objective was to obtain the heart of the Ouroboros, a mythic-grade annihilation factor sealed in the basement of the Garden's library, along with information on the facilities where the other pieces of the Ouroboros were kept. We are presently still attempting to locate her, but her current whereabouts remain unknown."

This explanation was given by a girl with dark hair and dark eyes, her gaze cool, and her expression betraying not a hint of emotion. The girl was dressed from head to toe in the monotonous uniform of a personal attendant.

Her name was Kuroe Karasuma—and she served the head of Void's Garden.

Right now, she stood ramrod straight behind Mushiki's back, above the sideways-looming skyscraper.

"I see...," uttered the low voice of a man.

The next moment, the world to Mushiki's right pulsated slightly, spreading out and zooming in.

Emerging in its place was a frightening scene bathed in red moonlight. A row of dead trees. Barren earth. A single Western-style building, with an endless bundle of spires, emanating a bewitching glow.

And a tall man sitting back in a chair.

Though appearance was no guarantee of a mage's true age, he looked to be around forty years old. His eyes were shielded by rainbow-colored glasses, and he wore a long cloak.

Despite the immense distance between them, Mushiki had no difficulty making out his voice and appearance.

Eishuu Gurendoh—the headmaster of the mage-training institute Ember's Peak.

"The Ouroboros. To think that sealed Mythologia could have been resurrected—and fused with a human no less... Do you have a photograph of this Clara Tokishima?"

"Yes," Kuroe responded, moving the fingers of her right hand as though swiping on a giant tablet screen.

Then, in the center of that huge space, an image filled the air.

A young woman in a flashy outfit, with pink hair and multiple earrings and ear cuffs, posing and winking to the camera as if taking a selfie.

Frankly speaking, that image was a far cry from the overall mood of this gathering.

"...Couldn't you have found a different picture?" Gurendoh grumbled.

"There *are* others," Kuroe said with a wave of her hand.

The next moment, the huge image projected in the center of the world was replaced with another, then another.

Clara in a peculiar outfit.

Clara cosplaying as a maid.

Clara's clothes being melted by a slime, the image a stone's throw away from having to be blurred out for decency's sake.

"Enough!" Gurendoh growled in resignation.

In the end, the first image had indeed been the most mature.

"Anything else of note?"

"Yes. Her Influenster ability converts fame and attention into magical energy. In other words, the more people who know about her and who are aware of her exploits, the greater her power increases."

"What a headache. So even if we exercise caution, that will only boost her powers?"

"That's right. However..." Kuroe paused for a moment, moving her hand once more and replacing the projected photograph with a short video clip.

"Hiya there! And we're back—it's Clara Channel Time! Are you having a ca-razy *day, my Claramates? Right then, so I'm thinking of running a little experiment today. Something called* Are Immortals Really Incapable of Dying?!*"*

The video continued, and the mage Clara Tokishima spoke to the audience amid the turmoil on display in a lighthearted manner, complete with exaggerated reactions and gestures.

Watching her, Gurendoh raised a quizzical eyebrow.

"...What's *this*?"

"A video, uploaded to the mage-exclusive video website MagiTube just a few hours ago," Kuroe said, her eyes downcast.

Right. Even with everything that had happened, despite her attack on the Garden and her true identity coming to light, Clara continued to post new videos.

"Of course, we've asked the company responsible for managing the website to suspend her account, but it seems she keeps finding new ways to bypass our restrictions, either by creating new accounts or using those of her followers. It's a game of cat and mouse, I'm afraid," Kuroe explained.

Gurendoh rested a hand on his forehead as though battling a migraine. "...You're telling me that gamboling upstart prankster is a mythic-grade annihilation factor?"

"*How rude, judging others by their appearance,*" sounded a flat electronic voice.

The speaker's identity was soon revealed. Just as it had when Gurendoh first spoke, the scenery warped, the space to Mushiki's left pulsating and expanding.

Spreading out before him was a pixelated video game screen. In the center of that blinking, low-resolution landscape sat a man with somewhat gloomy eyes, hunched over on both knees.

Baito Shikimori, headmaster of the mage-training institute Twilight City. Though he looked young, like Gurendoh, he was another powerful mage fully qualified to attend this conference.

"*That girl is fused with the Ouroboros and has turned more than a hundred mages into Immortals to attack the Garden. That's all that matters. Unnecessary preconceptions can cloud one's judgment.*"

"I don't need *you* to tell me that. I'm not about to let my guard down, no matter the foe," Gurendoh grumbled back in mild irritation.

"*If I was to judge you by your appearance, I'd say you're a dubious-looking middle-aged man.*"

"And you're as garrulous as ever, I see."

"*I don't know what kind of look you're going for, but round sunglasses are taking it a bit too far, if you ask me.*"

"Are you ever going to learn when to drop it?!" Gurendoh exclaimed in exasperation.

On closer inspection, he seemed more than a little embarrassed, his cheeks having turned bright red.

Then, perhaps in response to this exchange, the space to the far right of Mushiki's vision stirred slightly.

The scenery reminded him of the interior of a grand Japanese-style building. The sliding fusama doors, installed in several layers, opened quickly one after the other, revealing a bamboo blind at the very end of the building.

Behind it, the silhouette of a figure leaning forward was faintly visible.

"…Whatever the case…," the woman's voice began from behind the screen.

She was Ao Fuyajoh, headmistress of the mage-training institute Hollow Arc.

"First of all, we should clarify where the responsibility for this debacle lies… Isn't that right, Rindoh?"

"…"

At this, the last person joining them flinched.

In appearance, she looked to be around thirteen or fourteen years old, with a fearless countenance and her hair tied in a bun behind her head. Her eyebrows, clearly defined as though to emphasize her strong willpower, were now twisted in a grim expression.

Her presence, here in this space, was highly unusual.

The reason for that was simple—she was the only figure here who was not the head of a mage-training institute.

As if to hammer home that point, she was seated in what was possibly a plain conference room bathed exclusively in white. Only a single chair filled that wide expanse.

The girl's name was Rindoh Shionji, and she was a student at Shadow Tower.

There were two main reasons why she, a student, had been invited to this meeting.

The first was that she was the great-great-granddaughter and a direct descendent of the Tower's former headmaster Gyousei Shionji.

The second was that so many mages at the Tower had been turned into Immortals during the previous incident.

"It's true that Saika let Clara Tokishima slip away... But that was only because she was immortal, right? The Garden was attacked without warning by more than a hundred enemies, but Saika managed to fend them off. That feat should be worthy of praise, not denounced."

"So? What of the Tower?" Ao continued, moving as though she were peering at Rindoh's face. "Are we to believe that no one noticed anything unusual ahead of time, not even with more than a hundred mages—the headmaster included—being turned into Immortals?"

"W-well...," Rindoh stammered at this pointed remark.

Ao, however, looked to be in no mood to lower her weapons. "Tell me, Rindoh. When did your dear old grandfather stoop to becoming a filthy Immortal? Or do you mean to tell me you don't even know that...? Tch. What a mess old Shionji has gotten himself caught up in. Incompetence is one thing, but getting turned into an annihilation factor's pawn and threatening the whole human race? He would have been better off choosing death."

"..."

Until now, Rindoh had been staring down at her feet in shame, when she suddenly looked up. "As the acting representative of Shadow Tower...I'm truly, very sorry. I'm terribly ashamed for what's happened. I will accept any criticism, any condemnation... But please! I beg of you, take back that insult to my great-great-grandfather's name...!"

Her voice resonated with quiet anger. Her hands were trembling slightly, and her face was dripping with cold sweat.

It was little wonder. Of course she resented those remarks—but they had come from the head of another mage-training school. Ao was too powerful an opponent for her to dare express an opinion like this directly. It was only natural that she was tense and filled with fear.

Yet Ao merely waved the fan clutched in her hand, chuckling in the face of Rindoh's determination.

A shadow flickered from behind the bamboo blind.

"Insult?" she responded. "What a curious thing to say. Does the

Tower consider it an insult to state the simple fact of the matter? Then what *should* I say? That Gyousei Shionji, your institute's headmaster, was a fool for failing to notice a surprise attack coming from one of his own students? Or perhaps he had some ulterior motive involving Clara Tokishima? Either way, he ought to be dead by now—yet he's still alive and well."

"…!"

Rindoh, unable to stand this anymore, pushed her chair back and jumped quickly to her feet.

Then she crouched low as two bright, gleaming patterns appeared over her hands and shoulders.

Her world crest—a pattern that emerged whenever a modern-day mage used one of their substantiation techniques.

"Second Substantiation: Meteoric Stria…!"

As Rindoh said those words, a rugged long sword appeared by her waist.

Her second substantiation—the second of her unique manifestation techniques—transformed mana into matter.

Rindoh took a battle stance against Ao.

"…Oh?" Ao's tone underwent a dangerous transformation. "What is the meaning of this? Even here, it's no joke to point a weapon at someone. Or have you, too, been taken in by the Ouroboros? I suppose it's like they say, you can't fight your own blood."

"…Don't you dare say another word!" Rindoh cried in anger as she hit the ground running.

She must have been using some kind of magic technique, as she sped toward Ao with the speed of a flying bullet.

"Hmm…" Her target, however, wasn't the slightest bit flustered.

With a wave of her folding fan, a blue will-o'-the-wisp shaped like a giant bird appeared before the bamboo blind.

Rindoh continued her approach, while Ao waited to intercept it. In just a few brief moments, the two substantiations would collide.

But—

"Lady Saika," Kuroe urged.

"…Hmm."

The next moment, Mushiki waved his hand, sending a skyscraper falling from the sky to separate the two.

"Eeep...?!"

"Oh?"

The gigantic structure all but grazed against Rindoh's nose as it pierced the ground, shattering the boundaries of the world before eventually melting away into the air.

"Calm down, both of you," Mushiki said in an effort to placate them—the voice emanating from his throat clearly not that of a man.

But that was also as it should be.

Because right now, Mushiki *wasn't* himself.

Long, shimmering hair covered his head and shoulders.

His facial features were neat and orderly, perfectly arranged according to the golden ratio.

And enshrined in the middle of it were a pair of astonishing-colored eyes.

Yes. He wasn't the male high school student Mushiki Kuga, but rather Saika Kuozaki, headmistress of the mage-training institute Void's Garden.

"...Rindoh," Mushiki called out.

"Y-yes...?" she replied in a weak voice.

"I understand how you feel, but Ao isn't your enemy. I ask you, please don't bare your weapon here."

"Ah... S-sorry...!" Rindoh, who had seemed possessed earlier, bowed obediently, and deactivated her world crest and sword.

Next, Mushiki looked at Ao. "You too. You always go too far. Apologize to Rindoh," he instructed.

"Yes, I said too much. I'm sorry." Ao nodded indifferently.

"...Not at all," Rindoh replied with a bitter expression. She still looked a little agitated, but she seemed to understand at least that her behavior had posed a serious problem.

It was perhaps going too far to say that the matter was settled, but both Rindoh and Ao seemed to have calmed down for the time being.

"Seriously, cut it out. Fellow mages quarreling now? What's to become of us?" Gurendoh interjected.

"*Oh, it's fine, isn't it? So long as they only go at it* here. *I'm kinda* interested. I mean, a young mage challenging Ao Fuyajoh? Are you kidding?" Shikimori countered.

"Why you…"

If left unchecked, these two would no doubt start another argument, so Mushiki let out an audible cough to catch everyone's attention.

"In that case, let's discuss concrete countermeasures… The Ouroborus–Clara Tokishima hybrid must be defeated. I'll need you all to lend me your strength."

Close to sixty minutes later, the meeting came to an end.

To be honest, there was a lot that Mushiki couldn't fully grasp, but he did his best to maintain a composed expression at all times. As they had both agreed earlier, whenever he had trouble answering a given question, he would give an exaggerated nod and turn the discussion over to Kuroe.

He had been at the Garden for only a short period of time, so he couldn't be expected to respond perfectly to every question. His principal responsibility here was to appeal to the heads of the other schools and convince them that Saika was alive and well.

"…That's about everything. Thank you all again, everyone," Mushiki said at last, looking at the others now that the discussions were concluded.

That was a de facto declaration of adjournment, and the heads of the other schools responded in tacit understanding.

"Ah. I'll be off, then… Hopefully next time it will be about a more peaceful matter," Gurendoh said with a snap of his fingers—and with that, both he and the red space that he was inhabiting disappeared like a rising mist, leaving only a view of a simple conference room.

"Me too. Send me the details later, m'kay?"

Next was Shikimori, his electronic voice blending into static that soon consumed his image.

"…O-oh…" Rindoh watched in awe before noticing Mushiki's gaze and jumping back in fright. "Um, I'll excuse myself, too."

"Thank you for taking the time to join us."

"Not at all… I'm sorry for causing such a scene," Rindoh said with an apologetic look. Then, glancing back and forth at the spaces that Gurendoh and Shikimori had been occupying until just a moment earlier, she asked, "...U-um, sorry. Is it okay if I leave normally?"

"Of course." Mushiki nodded in response to this awkward question. Perhaps she thought she had to make some dramatic exit, too?

Her consternation was cute to watch, and Mushiki could feel his face relaxing into a smile—but he fought to hold it back. If he laughed here, no doubt he would leave her feeling even more self-conscious.

"Good-bye then...," Rindoh said with a humble bow before awkwardly turning to leave.

But then, as if suddenly struck by a question, she stopped, glancing back at him. "Is my grandfather—Gyousei Shionji, I mean... Is he still alive?"

"Yes. In his current state, he won't die even if you kill him."

It was Kuroe who answered. The remark could have been taken as a joke or sarcasm, but there was no hint of levity in her voice. It was, ultimately, just a simple statement of fact.

At this, Rindoh gave an uneasy frown. "I know this is a lot to ask, but might I be permitted to see—"

"If you just want to see him, I wouldn't recommend it. Especially if you want to maintain your respect for the man he once was."

"..."

Rindoh clenched her teeth and turned to face Mushiki.

"...I'll do my best, for what little it's worth. I'll stop the Ouroboros—I'll stop Clara Tokishima," she said as if to affirm her resolve.

Then, with one last glare at Ao, she offered Mushiki a deep bow and made her exit, disappearing into thin air.

And so there was only one figure left—Ao Fuyajoh, who was watching from behind her bamboo blind.

"Ah, youth," she said with a wave of her fan. "Vivacious anger when faced with the absurdities of the world—now that's a feeling I haven't felt in a long time. No... Maybe I should say I've grown accustomed to them. I envy her a little."

"Envy? You don't *sound* jealous," Mushiki admonished her with a dour look.

Ao shrugged. "I have no ill feelings toward her."

"Is that so?" Mushiki asked, her eyes narrowed.

It was a special talent, in a sense, being able to say all that to someone to whom you held no ill will toward.

"Yes, of course," Ao answered with a quick nod. "It's just…old Shionji is another matter entirely. For *him*, I've nothing but contempt and disgust. For someone responsible for one of our academies to throw himself on the mercy of an annihilation factor and attack humans… Death would be too good for him. But there's the problem—we can't even kill him."

"…Don't hold it against him too much. Mythologia aren't like regular annihilation factors. They exist in a realm that transcends common sense. You know that firsthand, yes?"

"…"

Ao pursed her lips at Mushiki's last remark.

He was referring to something that Kuroe had briefed him on prior to the meeting. As a mage, Ao had once been involved in the subjugation of another mythic-grade annihilation factor alongside Saika, the Leviathan.

"…That's precisely why I feel the way I do. We must *never* lose to those annihilation factors. No matter what they do. No matter what it takes… There's no meaning in a fight well fought, no value in praise. No medal for us mages, either. What we need to do is achieve concrete results… Isn't that right, Saika?"

"Ao…?"

Sensing a deep undercurrent of hatred in her voice, Mushiki arched an eyebrow.

"…?"

In the next moment, as though sensing something was off, Ao tilted her head. "…You *are* Saika, aren't you?"

"…?!"

Mushiki's heart skipped a beat.

…She couldn't possibly have seen through to his true identity, could she?

With an astonishing degree of concentration and his paranoid powers of observation, Mushiki had been doing his utmost to reproduce Saika's mannerisms and voice. That said, there was no such thing as perfection in this world (except for Saika's good looks, that is). Perhaps he had slipped up without even realizing it.

Obscured behind her bamboo blind, Ao's face was unreadable.

Mushiki glanced at Kuroe, imploring her to help.

"..."

Kuroe, however, said nothing, and merely watched their exchange without betraying a single thought of her own.

For a moment, he thought she had given up—but no.

She was simply demonstrating with her body how the attendant *Kuroe Karasuma* would respond in this situation.

And so Mushiki pursed his lips. "...It seems that I've lost my sense of humor since we last saw each other. Or have I become so beautiful that you hardly recognize me?"

"..." After a long moment, Ao let out a small sigh. "Apologies. I said something strange."

"No, don't let it worry you."

Mushiki spoke measuredly, doing his best not to betray the turmoil in his chest.

"I'm glad we had a chance to talk again," Ao continued as she tried to collect herself. "If not for this meeting, I would have given you a better welcome."

"Ah…yes. How about I invite you to tea next time? The best tea available, with cupcakes."

"Oh-ho, I look forward to it. Let's make it a celebration after defeating the Ouroboros." Then, changing the topic, Ao asked, "Is Ruri well? That girl hardly ever writes to me."

Mushiki felt his eyebrows almost twitch at the sound of that name.

That was only natural. Ruri Fuyajoh, the student in question, was his younger sister.

Then again, it *was* perfectly natural that she would come up in any conversation with Ao.

After all, they both shared the same surname.

Much to Mushiki's surprise, the Fuyajohs, his own maternal relatives, seemed to be a well-regarded and prestigious family in the magic world.

In other words, Ao was a blood relative of both Ruri and himself, though he wasn't sure of the precise nature of their relationship.

"Oh, don't worry. She seems to be enjoying herself with every passing day... Her abilities are amazing, too. She's already an S-ranked mage. And I enjoy having her around."

"Hmm... I see," Ao mumbled meaningfully. "Then it's fine. Seeing how she half forced herself into the Garden, it wouldn't do if she didn't achieve results," she said, her face filled with deep emotion as she looked up at Mushiki. "Yes, I truly am glad you made it in time."

"Hmm?"

"It's nothing." Ao hid her face behind her fan as though to brush aside Mushiki's remark.

Then again, that was hardly necessary as her face was already hidden behind a bamboo blind.

"Well then, it's time I go, too."

"Ah... See you again soon."

"Yes... We can't allow a mythic-grade annihilation factor to roam the streets. We'll bring it down... I'll do everything in my power."

With those final words, the space around Ao disappeared, as though consumed by blue flames.

...Finally, only Mushiki and Kuroe remained.

"...Phew."

A few seconds after realizing they were now alone, Mushiki let out a tired sigh, the tension built up inside him unraveling.

At the same time, the horizontal skyscraper on which he was sitting vanished, the space around him returning to its original form.

The two were in a bleak conference room—awfully empty in appearance, no doubt on account of the sparse furniture and decoration.

"Well done," Kuroe said appreciatively from behind him.

Mushiki turned around and gave a forced smile. "...I hope it went all right. She seemed a little suspicious there at the end."

"Headmistress Fuyajoh is always like that. Even while Lady Saika was still in her prime, she would often say suggestive insinuations and throw barbs for no apparent reason."

"...I see."

Once more, Mushiki let out an awkward sigh.

"But still—that's really bad for the heart."

As he spoke, he recalled the scene that until a moment ago had stretched out before him, and he glanced down to scrutinize his right hand.

A space divided into five colors. The dispute between Rindoh and Ao. And Saika's towering skyscraper that had brought an end to it.

From Mushiki's standpoint, that scene of carnage could very well have ended with someone dying. Even now, his heart was still racing.

Kuroe, however, was calm. "Don't worry. As I explained earlier, no one was actually there. We asked them to stop because, yes, those two fighting would have certainly caused a problem, but even if it had come to bloodshed, they wouldn't have died."

Right. Everything that Mushiki had just seen had been simply a projection wrought by magic.

In other words, it was a magic-based remote conference. The rooms seemed to be designed through the application of a technique that changed the surrounding scenery in accordance with the individual accessing it.

"But part of our consciousness is still connected, right? Is that what you mean? Strong stimuli that would end up having a physical response?"

"It wouldn't *kill* them," Kuroe answered flatly.

"...Right," Mushiki responded, still uneasy.

Then again, this probably wasn't a big deal as far as she was concerned.

"Now then," she continued, changing the subject. "While our options are limited, our plan of action has been decided. For now, we must all do what we can."

"What we can...?"

"Yes. That means magic training in the meantime... For you to master Lady Saika's techniques, and to also handle your own techniques, it is imperative that you increase your magic level. Even if Clara

Tokishima is found, that knowledge won't do us much good if you cannot fight her properly." Kuroe paused for a moment, glancing at her watch. "Fortunately, the meeting ended ahead of schedule, so we have time to spare. If we leave now, we may be able to make it to your first class. Let's hurry along and get ready."

"Get ready?"

"Don't play dumb. We've done this countless time before."

Then, watching him through narrowed eyes, Kuroe wrapped her arms around Mushiki's neck and positioned her lips close to his ear.

"…Or would you rather I take the lead?" she whispered, her bewitching voice tickling his ear.

"…!"

Mushiki's breath caught in his throat.

She looked so different from her usual appearance as an attendant, her teasing tone calling to mind Saika's sensuality.

But that, too, wasn't at all surprising.

After all, Kuroe was, in fact, the real Saika Kuozaki herself.

Yes. There had never been a real Kuroe Karasuma anywhere in this world. She was a homunculus, an artificial body created to house Saika's soul.

About a month ago, the real Saika had been mortally wounded, and before slipping away for good, she had transferred her soul to this artificial body that went by the name Kuroe.

Simply put, two beings now existed side by side—Saika's body as merged with Mushiki, and Saika's soul dwelling within Kuroe's body.

When Kuroe had talked about *getting ready*, she meant for Mushiki to return to his original state.

In his current form, Mushiki was constantly radiating magical energy. When that amount underwent a rapid increase, his body would attempt to suppress the loss by entering a safe mode that consumed less energy— in other word's, Mushiki's original body.

And *this* was how to instigate it.

After all, magic was closely linked to the mind.

Essentially, when he entered a state of extreme arousal, the amount of magical energy being released would spike.

"Heh-heh, you're a naughty boy. Perhaps you're in need of a little disciplining?"

"A-ah... Ugh..."

So went Mushiki and Kuroe's exchange, both of them blushing as they talked.

"...Um, sorry. I forgot to ask you something. It's about the student Mushiki Kuga mentioned in the report..."

Suddenly, there was a rumbling at the end of the room, and the representative from the Tower, Rindoh Shionji, timidly reappeared.

"Ah."

"Er."

"...Huh?!"

As she took in the sight of Mushiki and Kuroe, her face instantly turned scarlet.

"Eeep! U-um, s-sorry! S-sorry for disturbing yoouuu!" Rindoh cried out, covering her mouth with her hands and disappearing again without a trace.

"..."

"..."

The two of them were left in stunned silence for a few moments, when—

"Ah..."

Mushiki's body faintly glowed, his appearance changing into that of an androgynous male high school student. He was back in his original form.

She had left just in the nick of time. If the transformation had taken place a few seconds earlier, Rindoh might have seen everything.

"...Do you perhaps like it when someone's watching?" Kuroe asked, squinting at him.

"You've got the wrong idea!" he couldn't help crying out.

Void's Garden, the mage-training institute located in Ohjoh City in Tokyo, was divided into five major areas.

The eastern precinct, where many of the research buildings were located.

The western precinct, where there was a high concentration of training facilities.

The southern precinct, full of dormitories and commercial facilities.

The northern precinct, occupied by Saika's mansion and other private amenities.

And the central precinct, where most of the school buildings were situated.

After leaving the special conference building located in the northern precinct, Mushiki and Kuroe made their way along the paved path down to the campus's central area.

As they approached, the road gradually grew in width, various buildings peeking out from behind the dense trees. Since they usually made their way to school from their dormitory in the southern precinct, it provided a refreshing change of scenery.

That, however, wasn't the only reason for the unfamiliar sights.

"…Right, the repairs aren't done yet, huh?" Mushiki, back in his original body, murmured as he walked along the pavement.

Several of the roads and buildings had collapsed, with work crews busy restoring them.

All probably lingering effects from the previous incident.

"It looks like it," Kuroe responded from next to him.

In tone and atmosphere, she had reverted to the perfect coolheaded attendant. Mushiki would have liked it if she spoke more casually with him, but they couldn't afford to let anyone learn her true identity, so she typically played the role of Kuroe Karasuma with great aplomb.

"It's fairly common for the facilities to sustain some degree of damage during exhibition matches, but the scale was so large that it will take some time to repair. Though if we still had Silvelle, the work might proceed a little more efficiently."

"Ah…"

Mushiki sighed at the sound of that name.

Silvelle—the artificial intelligence in charge of security and management at the Garden.

Just like the students of the Tower, she had fallen into Clara's hands. In short, she had been turned against them, and so the Garden could be said to have bared its fangs on its own staff and students. Mushiki felt a chill run down his spine when he stopped to wonder how he had managed to survive it all.

It ought to be possible to restore Silvelle as she was an AI...but even now, several days after the incident, there had been no indication that anyone planned to.

"Silvelle hasn't been fixed up yet, huh? It feels a little lonely without her."

At that moment, Mushiki's eyes widened in surprise.

A familiar figure was walking down the path, straight for them.

"...? What is it, Mushiki?"

"Er, is that...?"

He pointed ahead with a blank stare.

She was a beautiful young woman, perhaps around eighteen years old. She walked slowly, her long silver hair almost touching the ground and her ample breasts on the verge of bursting out from her clothing as they swayed with each step.

There could be no doubt about it. It was a three-dimensional projection of the Garden's management AI Silvelle, the kind she used when communicating with people.

"..."

She pushed on ahead, oblivious to Mushiki and Kuroe, seemingly muttering something under her breath.

Well, Mushiki reasoned, she was only a projection, so there was little chance of their colliding.

Yet—

"Huh?"

The next moment, Mushiki gasped.

The reason was simple. His fingers, stretched out in front of him, had pressed up against Silvelle's chest.

"...?!"

A second later, Silvelle jerked back. A faint tremor passed through her, from her chest all the way to Mushiki's fingers.

"...Wh-wh-wh-wh-wh-what...?"

A faint voice like the buzz of a mosquito emanated from her throat.

Mushiki furrowed his brow in confusion.

"She's got a physical form…? Hold on. What's going on—"

"Mushiki. Please lower your hand."

"Ah."

Only after Kuroe had spoken did he realize what he was still doing. Flustered, he hurried to put his hand away.

"S-sorry," he stammered.

"…N-no… It's okay… Eeep…," Silvelle responded in a voice so small that he might not have heard it if he hadn't been paying attention. "I—I was just startled, that's all… I'm sorry you had to touch something so plain… I was lost in thought…," she said in a strained, anxiety-ridden voice.

For a moment, Mushiki thought she was angry at him for his disrespectful behavior…but apparently not. Rather, she seemed quite unaccustomed to brushing things off with a casual laugh.

Watching her, Mushiki finally realized this woman wasn't the Silvelle he knew.

Her features and stature were exactly like the AI, but her clothes, facial expressions, and overall atmosphere were simply too different.

Silvelle had worn a white robe and always had a gracious, saintly smile—perfectly befitting the self-proclaimed big sister figure she endeavored to be.

The girl in front of him now, however, was dressed in a frilly gothic Lolita-style dress that covered her body almost completely. She had a severe stoop, and her long bangs partly obscured her face. Her eyesight didn't seem particularly great, either, as she was wearing a pair of narrow framed glasses. In one hand, she grasped a parasol, her shoulders slumped forward as though to keep them from being exposed to the sun.

If Silvelle was yang, this woman was yin—her aura was practically the polar opposite of the AI's.

Kuroe spoke up to address his confusion: "Mushiki. While they may look very similar, this is not the administrative AI Silvelle."

"Ah…right. I guessed as much," Mushiki said, still staring at the woman. "But in that case—"

"This is Hildegarde Silvelle," Kuroe continued, anticipating his next question. "She is the head of the Garden's technical department and the creator of the AI Silvelle. She is also one of our knights."

"...! Silvelle's...creator...?! And a knight?!" Mushiki exclaimed, his eyes opening wide in shock.

Hildegarde's shoulders trembled slightly. The next moment—

"Uh, hee-hee..."

She let out an awkward, evasive chuckle.

Yep, Mushiki had a feeling that she wasn't used to laughing in front of others.

"...Um, Kuroe? Is she really a knight?" Mushiki whispered so that Hildegarde wouldn't overhear.

The knights of Void's Garden were the school's strongest mages and a special task force under Saika's direct control.

It probably wasn't a polite thing to say out loud, but Hildegarde seemed like a far cry from the other knights he knew.

Kuroe seemed to sense his misgivings. "To be appointed as a knight, a high level of proficiency as a mage, a proven track record, and Lady Saika's endorsement are required. That is not necessarily determined solely by combat ability... In one sense, being the creator of an AI responsible for the Garden's security, you can say that she defends our students from more harm than anyone else."

"I see..."

Mushiki felt ashamed for being shallow-minded and simultaneously was reminded of Saika's depth of knowledge. He lowered his gaze, doing his best to keep tears from welling up in his eyes.

"E-eh...? What's wrong...?" Hildegarde asked, her head tilted in confusion.

"I-it's nothing..."

There was no way he could tell her the truth.

Hoping to distract her, he asked her something that had been bothering him for a while: "Um, right. Why does Silvelle want everyone to call her *Sis*?"

It was a question that he had already received an answer to, but ultimately, he was merely hoping to change the subject.

AI Silvelle had a strong desire to be treated as an older sister. Not only the students but the teaching staff as well addressed her as *Sis*. In fact, she wouldn't even respond to questions if you called her by any other name, and she tended to get sulky to boot. As an administrative AI, her attitude could often be a bit of a problem.

"...!" Hildegarde trembled uneasily. "I—I don't know..."

"Huh? But you made her, right...? And she looks just like you..."

"Ugh..." Hildegarde's face warped in alarm. "I don't know... I added a self-learning runtime, and before I knew it...she became the big sister of all humankind? I don't get it, not one bit... Besides... Having a visual projection while communicating is all well and good, but why did she model herself after *me*...? It's so embarrassing... I wish she wouldn't..." She fell silent and was on the verge of bawling her eyes out.

"Mushiki." Kuroe spoke up. "Don't bother her so much. Knight Hildegarde is extremely talented, but she's also extremely sensitive."

"Ah... S-sorry...," Mushiki apologized.

"I-it's okay...," Hildegarde said, though she seemed far from it.

Kuroe cleared her throat. "But this *is* unusual," she began, changing the topic. "It's rare to see you out and about so early in the morning, Knight Hildegarde."

"...Ah, well, er, it's about Silvelle's...recovery..."

Mushiki couldn't quite make out the second half of her halting response, but he understood enough to know that she was on her way somewhere to help reactivate the administrative AI.

"So it'll still take some more time?" Kuroe asked.

"Ah...y-yes...," Hildegarde answered with a weak nod. "...The Ouroboros...right...? It's a mythic-class annihilation factor... Well, Silvelle's core makes use of several living parts...and they've been rendered immortal from the Ouroboros's ability. It will be...practically impossible to restore her to the way she was before... All we can do is rebuild her based on an external backup... In the meantime, campus security is in the hands of conventional AIs and humans...," she explained in a roundabout manner.

Her voice was so quiet, and she spoke so fast, that Mushiki couldn't fully catch the gist of her explanation, but in any event, it was clear it would take some time to fully restore the AI.

"...Right..." He nodded; his voice subdued.

"Wh-what...?" Hildegarde asked fearfully.

"No...I just thought it would be lonely, not being able to talk to the old Silvelle anymore. I didn't know her for that long, but she was a huge help..."

"..."

Hildegarde's eyes widened in surprise at his remark.

That moment, the bell sounded from the central school building. It looked like they had spent more time talking than Mushiki had expected.

"Oh, it's time. We have class, Knight Hildegarde. Please excuse us. Let's hurry along, Mushiki."

"Ah, right. Excuse me. Sorry again for bumping into you."

"Eh...ah...um...w-wait, please." Just as Mushiki and Kuroe were about to leave, Hildegarde called out to them.

Mushiki stopped. "...? Yes? What is it?"

"Um...I know I said there are some biological parts...but that doesn't change the fact that Silvelle is an AI... Her structure is fundamentally different from that of a human being... And with the external back-ups, well, there are multiple memory units..."

"Huh?"

Mushiki tilted his head, unsure what she was getting at.

"U-uh...," she stammered, falling silent.

Instead, it was Kuroe who offered a supplementary explanation: "In short, though it will indeed be difficult to restore the AI Silvelle completely, rest assured that she won't be an entirely different person."

"...Y-yes." Hildegarde nodded. "Sh-she's a little strange, that AI... but she's my little girl... Thank you for looking out for her..."

"Not at all. Thank *you* for making her."

"Ah...um... Tee-hee-hee..."

In response to Mushiki's show of thanks, Hildegarde gave an awkward smile, but she *did* seem happy to hear them.

◇

Void's Garden may have been a mage-training institute, but as a place with teachers and students where knowledge was taught, it wasn't all that much different from schools on the outside.

In that regard, the schedule was no exception. The day began with homeroom, followed by periods 1 through 4 in the morning, a break for lunch, then periods 5 and 6 in the afternoon.

All of this was to say…the fact that Mushiki and Kuroe could hear the bell from outside the school building meant that they were very, very late.

"Ah, Kuga, Karasuma. Good morning."

No sooner had the two of them entered the classroom than a female student with soft facial features and her pretty hair tied back neatly in a bun called out to them—their classmate Hizumi Nagekawa.

"Morning, Nagekawa," Mushiki responded with a wave.

"Good morning," Kuroe said.

As far as he could see, there were only students present in the classroom. Everyone was either busy talking with friends or preparing for the day's classes. It seemed that they'd slipped in between homeroom and first period. It was a shame that they hadn't arrived in time to have their attendance recorded, but it was probably for the best that they hadn't barged into the room in the middle of class.

"You're late, you two," came a sharp voice.

In contrast to Hizumi, the individual who spoke this time was a young woman with a determined look to her face, and her long hair tied up in twin ponytails.

Ruri Fuyajoh—Mushiki's younger sister, the one whose name had come up in the conversation with Ao.

"You're a mess. Don't you have any idea what it means to be a mage…? Not that I'm acknowledging you as one or anything, you hear me?!" she said, adding the second part in a panic.

More than a month had passed since Mushiki had enrolled at the Garden, but Ruri was still intent on getting him to give up on becoming a mage.

Whenever the matter came up between them, the conversation would always turn sour. Mushiki gave her a wry smile, deliberately avoiding the topic as he took his seat.

"Ah, sorry, Ruri," he said. "Something important came up."

"Something important? And *what* exactly was it?"

"Um...well, you know."

He could hardly tell her that he had been attending a conference for principals of mage-training institutes in Saika's place. He glanced over at Kuroe, looking for help.

At that, Ruri gave a puzzled look—then, as though in sudden realization, she jumped back.

"C-come to think of it, you came to school with Kuroe, didn't you?! What were you two even doing?!" she demanded, her cheeks turning crimson as she pointed back and forth between the two of them.

Mushiki's eyes widened in alarm at this misunderstanding. "N-n-no, we didn't do anything!"

"...Really?"

"Really!"

"...She didn't hug you from behind and whisper seductively into your ear?"

"...No."

Mushiki averted his gaze at that pointed accusation, spoken as though she had literally witnessed just that.

Judging from her behavior, it was probably just a coincidence that her remarks were so close to the truth... Her intuition, however, could be frighteningly astute.

"Why are you talking like that?! Hey! Look at me!" Ruri demanded, grabbing him by the shoulders and shaking him back and forth.

"N-no...it really isn't like that! Right, Kuroe?!" he cried, beseeching her to back him up.

Then, with a cute expression, the kind that would normally never cross her features, she shyly lowered her gaze. "But it is... It's fine to admit it, Mushiki."

"Muuushiiikiii?!"

"W...what?!"

Ruri's eyes were on fire at Kuroe's response.

Right. Saika usually played the part of a cool and collected maid, but she had a bit of a mischievous side, too. It really was adorable.

However, given the current situation, he had no time to appreciate her playfulness. Ruri was becoming increasingly incensed.

"What's the meaning of this, Mushiki?! What have you been doing all morning…?! Huh?! No, don't tell me…*from last night?!* You mean you were both late because you didn't get enough sleep?! Arrrggghhh! You idiot! Idiiiooot! You said you'd marry *me* when we grew up!"

"C-calm down, Ruri…!" Hizumi intervened. "Hold on, what did you just say?!"

"…Huh?" Ruri suddenly stopped moving.

Her eyes were spinning as she ruminated over her last sentence—and she turned instantly scarlet.

"…Mushiki, did you hear that just now?"

"Huh? About marriage? I mean, kids make silly promises all the time, it—"

"Ugh! Nggghhh!"

He realized that he should have just played dumb, but the question had come so suddenly that he had ended up answering her honestly.

Ruri's face continued to turn an even deeper shade of red when she grabbed his arm, braced her legs, and put him in a joint lock.

"…?! …?!"

Mushiki's limbs tightened up, leaving him unable to control his own body. He could hear a faint scream echoing from his throat semiconsciously.

"That won't do, Knight Fuyajoh. Please calm down."

"Th-that's right. You should let Kuga—"

"If you want to incapacitate him, you have to wrap your arm properly around his neck."

"Karasuma?!" Hizumi cried back. Evidently, that hadn't been what she had meant.

But perhaps realizing that she had gone too far, or perhaps satisfied with Ruri's reaction, Kuroe sighed softly, then moved to tap Ruri on the shoulder.

"I was just kidding. I happened to bump into Mushiki on my way to class."

"...R-really...?"

While it may have been Ruri's own comment about marriage that was the direct cause behind her attempt to throttle him, Kuroe's concession had seemed to be enough to calm her down.

At last, the strength ebbed from her arms, and Mushiki fell helplessly to the floor, staggering back to his feet after a few seconds.

"A-are you all right? Mushiki...?" Hizumi asked.

"I-I'm fine..."

Having finally regained her composure, Ruri reached out to him awkwardly. "...Sorry about that. I got a bit carried away."

"A bit...?" Mushiki echoed with a forced smile, but nonetheless, he took her hand and got back on his feet.

Those hands, which she used in battle daily in her role as a mage of the Garden, possessed both the delicateness of a young woman and the hardiness of a fierce warrior.

The next moment—

"...Hmm?"

Mushiki's eyes widened in shock.

An unfamiliar thing had just flown in through a gap in the classroom windows.

It was a small bird, its feathers flickering like flames—or perhaps it would be more accurate to say that it *was* a flame in the shape of a bird? It fluttered through the air, holding what looked like a tiny letter in its beak.

"What's that...?"

Drawn by Mushiki's gaze and voice, the others quickly noticed the small visitor, too, each looking in its direction and exclaiming in their own distinctive way.

"...A familiar? That's a rare sight...," Ruri said with a frown when the bird dropped its letter into the palm of her hand.

With that, the creature melted away into the air, having fulfilled its role.

"...It's for me?"

Curious, she scrutinized it. Written on the front in neat letters was *Ms. Ruri Fuyajoh.*

Seeing all this for the first time, Mushiki was beyond impressed.

"Wow. So this is how mages exchange letters, huh?"

"No it isn't," Ruri snapped back.

"Huh?" he gawked in response.

"A long time ago, maybe, but these days, the normal thing to do is to use email or a mage-exclusive messaging app. It's faster, easier, and more reliable, right? And there's no need to waste magic to actually *send* anything."

"Ah...that makes sense."

Come to think of it, Saika had said something along those lines before—that among traditional mages, there were those who still liked to do things the old-fashioned way.

"Well, I'm not saying there aren't any advantages whatsoever. If it's just a small charm, you can deliver the actual item, and of course, you don't leave any record of your exchanges on some server. And...well, sometimes people have reactions like you did just now, too..."

"My reaction?"

"When you saw the familiar bring the letter, you thought to yourself: *Wow!* Right? Basically, it looks cool."

"Because it looks cool... That's it?"

"It's really important to look cool while using magic. I mean, magic and the spirit are closely intertwined. Even *you* think fancy-looking techniques are better than weird ones, right? And that kind of feeling can greatly affect a spell's output. Your self-awareness, your self-confidence—they can help you use amazing techniques... So that's why familiars are still used for important messages, or for notifying people of formal events."

"I see..." Mushiki nodded in understanding. "Thank you, Ruri. That was very enlightening."

"Heh-heh. Don't mention it... What?"

At that moment, she jolted back in alarm as though suddenly

realizing something. "What do you think you're doing, learning all this?! I'm not here to teach you!"

"You're all over the place, Ruri...," Hizumi said with a nervous smile, her gaze shifting to the letter still in her friend's hand. "But more importantly, what does the letter say?"

"Hmm...? Ah, right. I think it's from the family head..."

She opened the seal, pulling out a sheet of writing paper. As she began to read the letter—

"Wh-wh-what...?!"

Her hands began to tremble, and she let out a curdling scream: "Nggghhh?! Whaaaaaat?! Arrrggghhh!"

"R-Ruri...?!"

"What happened...?!"

Mushiki and the others were taken aback by her sudden change of emotion. The next moment, Ruri slammed the letter down on the desk in front of her, not understanding what was going on.

"I don't... I don't get it! *Why?!* And out of nowhere...?!" she exclaimed, pointing at the letter for the others to see.

Mushiki looked down and read the message.

"I-is that...?!"

"H-huh...?!"

"...Hmm."

And like Ruri, they frowned in alarm and dismay.

But those weren't unreasonable responses. No doubt anyone would be flustered if they had received the same kind of letter.

On the paper, in neat and tidy handwriting, was the following:

Dear Ruri Fuyajoh,
Your forthcoming marriage has been finalized. I offer you my warmest congratulations.
Please quickly return to the main house to hold the ceremony.
Ao Fuyajoh

Chapter 2
The Witch Conquers Neptune's Fortress, Deep in the Sea

"Mushiki."

"…"

"Mushiki."

"…"

"Ah, how unexpected. Lady Saika is wearing a kimono of all things."

"Huh? Wh-where?!"

Mushiki snapped awake at these words, still reverberating in his eardrums.

Yet it wasn't Saika in a kimono who greeted him, but rather Kuroe with an unamused expression.

Well, that was only natural. Saika's body was fused with his own. So as long as he was here, there was no way that she could be present.

"So you *can* hear me. I've been calling out to you again and again," Kuroe said with a slight pout.

Mushiki lowered his head in apology. "…Sorry. I guess I kind of blanked out."

"Yet you still responded to Lady Saika's name."

"You can still notice a huge explosion nearby even when you're in a daze, right?"

"We're handling explosives?" Kuroe sighed deeply.

But that turn of phrase wasn't entirely wrong. Saika Kuozaki in a kimono...would probably have the destructive power of around two and half kilotons of TNT. That sight would be so dangerous, in fact, that its use would likely be restricted by international treaties.

"You're thinking of something stupid again, aren't you?"

"What? No way."

Mushiki shook his head without a moment's hesitation.

Sure, he *had* been mulling over how Saika would look in a kimono, but those were far from stupid thoughts.

Both he and Kuroe were in their usual classroom—Room 2-A. It was currently lunchbreak, and most of their fellow students had gone outside.

"...So what were you thinking about?"

"That it might be necessary to institute a treaty to regulate the use of Saika in a kimono—"

"Not that," Kuroe interrupted him. "Before that."

"Ah..." Mushiki let out a melancholy sigh while glancing at a nearby seat that had been left empty for the past few days without its usual occupant. "Well...Ruri, I guess."

"I thought so." Kuroe nodded in understanding.

...Did she feel a sense of relief hearing his response just now? *Thank goodness that pathetic monster still has a heart...?* But maybe he was just imagining things.

"It's already been five days since she got that letter... So what's going on?" he said with a worried frown.

For Mushiki, the goings-on of this classroom had become part of his everyday routine. But one thing was different to usual—Ruri was absent.

Of course, it wasn't like she had gone to the main Fuyajoh residence to obediently accept the marriage, but still...

Mushiki vaguely recalled their exchange five days earlier...

"You've gotta be kidding me!" Ruri cried out, slamming her fists down on the desk.

The bench top creaked from the force of the shock.

"What's this about marriage?! They send an old-fashioned letter out of the blue and decide this all by themselves...?! Old families are always like this!" She let out an indignant sigh, her whole body shaking.

Hizumi raised an eyebrow. "So...you're saying you didn't know anything about this, Ruri?"

"Of course not! I mean, I'm only sixteen!"

"Ah," Mushiki mouthed. Right. Under the current laws, she hadn't even reached marriageable age.

"Um...so what are you going to do?" Hizumi asked.

"Ignore it! Ignore it! I don't care what the main family says! No one has any right to decide this for me! Besides, I've already made up my mind about who I want to—" She stopped herself there.

"Huh?"

"...N-nothing!" she shouted, crumbling the letter into a ball and throwing it into the trash can at the front of the classroom.

She must have put too much strength into the throw, as the paper ball bounced right back out. Veins throbbing on her forehead, she moved to pick it up and dropped it back in the trash can. Even at a time like this, she managed to maintain her self-discipline.

"...But will that really work?" Kuroe asked with a hand on her chin.

"Will *what* work?"

"It's normally quite impossible to enter a marriage against one's will. And you're right, you're not old enough to marry in the first place... But this is Ao Fuyajoh we're talking about here, the head of the prestigious Fuyajoh family of mages. She may try to push through regardless. Is it something we should leave alone?"

"Ugh..."

Ruri must have realized the truth to Kuroe's comment, as she had broken out into a cold sweat. "R-right... I don't know what they're playing at, but maybe I should confront them about it...? I mean, it's crazy, being told you're getting married when you don't even know what's going on. I can't rule out the possibility of a stranger coming here claiming to actually *be* my husband..."

"Th-that's terrifying...," Hizumi said with an awkward smile.

It went *beyond* terrifying; that was for sure.

"But what exactly are you going to do about it?" Mushiki asked.

Ruri thought for a few moments before answering. "Well...I'll have to go and tell them what's what, in person. Nothing will change if I just write back and say no. Going there and making a scene will get my message across that much more clearly, right?" she said, waving her arm as though swinging a long sword.

Mushiki's mouth twitched. She was always quick to resort to violence.

"But does that mean you're actually going to go see them?" he asked.

"Well...the main house is where the family head is, so yeah."

"But maybe it's better not to go alone... Maybe I could—"

"No," she interrupted him, her expression and tone completely different from how they had been up till now.

"Huh...?"

It was a powerful rejection, coldhearted even. Mushiki widened his eyes at this uncharacteristic rebuff.

Seeing his reaction, Ruri shrugged slightly as if realizing how cold her voice had just turned.

"Ah...no... What I'm trying to say is that it won't do any good, having anyone else come with me! Not even you! I'll be back as soon as it's all sorted out, so just wait for me here...! No, scratch that! Just give up on becoming a mage already and leave the Garden, why don't you?!" She pointed a finger at him before turning to leave the room—then stopped as though suddenly remembering something. "Right. I should let Madam Witch know what I'm doing."

"..."

Mushiki and Kuroe exchanged silent looks.

Naturally. After all, Ruri was already facing Saika's body and consciousness.

"Ah, maybe now's not a good time?" Mushiki said.

"I'm afraid so. Lady Saika mentioned that she had some urgent business to attend to," Kuroe added.

"Wh-what's with you two? You're weirdly in sync..." Ruri made a dubious face, but quickly shook her head to regain her composure. "...Well, if she's busy, it can't be helped. Tell Madam Witch not to worry, and that I'll be right back. See you!"

"Ah, Ruri!" Mushiki called out behind her, but she had already dashed out of the classroom.

That was five days ago.

There was still no news from her, though she should have long since made her way to see the Fuyajoh family head.

Of course, they had tried to contact her. But whether by phone, email, or SNS, there was no response.

It would have been understandable if she had simply ignored the messages sent from Mushiki. She still hadn't accepted him as a mage yet, and she had only reluctantly shared her contact details at Hizumi's and Kuroe's urging. (Incidentally, ever since adding him as a friend on the messaging app, she has sent texts to him twice a day, once in the morning and at night—things like *Give up on being a mage!* or *Get out of the Garden!* or *Have you brushed your teeth?* or *Don't sleep in, you hear me?* complete with angry stickers and emojis.)

But the fact that she hadn't even responded to any of the messages from Saika was certainly out of the ordinary.

Either she was somewhere with no cellular reception, or she had lost her smartphone, or for whatever reason, she couldn't use it... In any case, it was clear that *something* was amiss. Mushiki tapped on his smartphone's screen in concern.

"Kuga..."

At that very moment, Hizumi called out to him.

He couldn't say she looked cheerful even as flattery. It wasn't hard to imagine that she was harboring the same worries he was.

"Nothing from Ruri?" she asked.

"...No. You neither?"

Hizumi nodded darkly. "Something must have happened. We can't even get in contact with her..." After a moment of thoughtful silence, she turned to Kuroe with a determined look. "Um, Karasuma? Will Madam Witch be coming to class today?"

"No. Lady Saika is taking the day off... But if there is anything you need, I can let her know," she answered, her expression unwavering.

"...The head of the Fuyajoh family is also the headmistress of the Ark, isn't she? So I was wondering if Madam Witch could ask about Ruri..."

Hizumi's face was tense, and there was a slight tremor in her voice. She knew it was an unreasonable request.

But even though she understood that, she still wanted to confirm Ruri's safety. The light burning in the depths of her eyes revealed her willpower.

Kuroe had both the capacity to recognize that determination and the generosity to heed it. Taking a deep breath, she answered, "I don't like interfering in family affairs, but Knight Fuyajoh is a student of the Garden. It wouldn't be strange for Lady Saika to be concerned about her welfare. I will ask her to reach out to the headmistress of the Ark."

"...! You will? Thank you!" Hizumi brightened up, taking Kuroe's hands in hers.

Kuroe wasn't normally the type to show much emotion, but her eyes widened slightly in surprise. It was a cute reaction.

"But please don't expect too much," she added. "For a mage, family is more than just a community. Not even Lady Saika can—"

But at that moment, she suddenly fell silent.

The reason for this soon became apparent.

A blue flame-shaped bird had just flown through a small gap in the windows to enter the classroom.

Yes. Ao's familiar, the same one that had delivered Ruri's letter five days earlier.

"...! Is that—"

"That bird...?!"

Mushiki and the others were wide-eyed with astonishment when the familiar, hovering in midair, dropped a small envelope on Ruri's desk and vanished in a burst of flame.

Only the letter was left in its place.

After exchanging glances with Kuroe and Hizumi, Mushiki reached out to take it.

There was no address on the envelope, but the name *Ruri Fuyajoh* was written as the sender on the back.

"It's from Ruri…?" he asked quizzically as he opened it.

There was no letter inside, just a small memory card.

"Huh…?"

"Let's see what's stored on it. I suppose a regular smartphone should work…?" Hizumi said, inserting it into her cell phone.

A few seconds later, a video popped up on the screen.

"*…Um, hello… I guess that's okay? It's me, Ruri Fuyajoh.*"

"Ruri…?!" Mushiki gasped.

His shock was warranted. After all, in the center of the video, Ruri was sitting on a chair in a drab room.

But she wasn't dressed in her usual Garden uniform. She wasn't even wearing regular clothes. She was dressed in a white outfit that called to mind a sailor's uniform.

Of course, since this was a video, their voices could not reach her. And so Ruri continued without responding to everyone's shock.

"*Whoever's watching this…you must be in my class, so please pass this on to the teacher.*" Then with a thin smile, she uttered the following unbelievable words: "*I, Ruri Fuyajoh, have been blessed with a good marriage partner, and we will soon be exchanging vows… As such, I will be dropping out of the Garden.*"

"Huh—"

"What…?"

"…"

Mushiki and Hizumi both gaped at this unexpected announcement. Kuroe refrained from gawking, but she nonetheless narrowed her eyes in suspicion.

Yet contrary to their expectations, Ruri continued with a bright look: "*I'll send all the necessary documents later… My days at the Garden were invaluable… My time with you all has been cut short, but thank you for everything… I wish you all the best for the future.*"

With that stock, bland closing remark, Ruri bowed.

And the video came to an end.

"..."

"..."

"..."

After a moment of stunned silence, Mushiki exchanged looks with Kuroe and Hizumi.

"...Clearly, something is up."

Kuroe was the first to speak; her brows were furrowed, her misgivings evident in her hushed tone.

Mushiki and Hizumi nodded in agreement.

"...Yeah. No matter how you look at it, something isn't right."

"Mm-hmm. The video raises a lot of questions..."

Come to think of it, there were many odd things with that recording.

First things first, it was unthinkable that Ruri would accept an arranged marriage so easily after making it clear that she was so strongly opposed to it. On top of that, why would she use Ao's familiar to send a message, and a video recording no less? It would have been much more natural if she had simply called them.

But above all else, there was one thing that could not be overlooked.

"...Impossible. She wouldn't send a message like that without saying anything to Saika."

"...She didn't mention Madam Witch at all."

"That's just it."

Mushiki and Hizumi both said simultaneously, while Kuroe likewise wore a look of amazement.

"I mean, you know Ruri."

"This *is* Ruri we're talking about."

"..."

Once more, the two of them spoke over each other with the same remarks.

Yes. There were several peculiarities with that video, but that was by far the one that stood out the most.

Assuming—just for argument's sake—that Ruri went to see the main family with the full intention of refusing the marriage but ended up falling head over heels in love with her prospective partner... In that case, she *might* hypothetically become open to the suggestion.

But getting married would have a profound impact on her life, especially as the Fuyajohs seemed to be a prominent and well-respected family. They could have all sorts of peculiar customs. The option of dropping out of the Garden might have also potentially come up.

If the main family was located somewhere with poor cellular service, it wasn't unthinkable that she would contact them through a recorded video.

However.

However...

Even if they were to turn a blind eye to all those possibilities...

There was absolutely no way that Ruri Fuyajoh, the honorary president of the (unofficial) Saika Kuozaki Fan Club, wouldn't have uttered so much as a word about her dear Madam Witch...!

If she really did have to leave the Garden because of some unavoidable dilemma, she would have tearfully told them about her situation. She would have expressed her gratitude to Saika without end, reminisced about her memories of Saika, and would have sung a song that she had written herself with a video of Saika playing in the background, telling them how reluctant she was to let everything go. Then, at the end, sobbing uncontrollably, she would probably have had to be dragged off-screen.

"There's no way you could fit all that on a single memory card," Mushiki murmured.

"Mm-hmm. No doubt about it," Hizumi added.

"You're very confident." Kuroe sighed.

But even if she had followed a different line of reasoning, Kuroe had also deemed the recording to be incredibly suspicious. And so, clearing her throat to regain her composure, she began: "At first glance, this does look like Ruri. However, I don't think it would be impossible, either with magic or with technology, to forge a video of this kind... In addition, we cannot deny the possibility that Ruri herself is being manipulated in some way, or that she might have been brainwashed."

"What…?!"

"No…!"

Both Mushiki and Hizumi broke into stern frowns.

"Brainwashing… Would they really go that far?" Hizumi asked.

"It's only a possibility. However, Ruri is likely the greatest talent among the current members of the Fuyajoh clan. As the headmistress of her own school, I doubt it was the family head's intention to have her enrolled at a rival institute. It's possible that she is using this as an opportunity to take drastic action."

"…We need to go help her. Where's this head of the family located anyway?!" Mushiki demanded with a scowl.

Kuroe shook her head. "Calm down, Mushiki. It isn't going to be that easy."

"Why not?"

"The mansion of the main Fuyajoh family is situated within the mage-training institute Hollow Ark. So to get there, you would first need to board the Ark itself."

"Board the Ark…? So what's the problem? I know I'm still inexperienced as a mage, but it's not like students from other schools can't enter?"

A large number of students from the Tower had entered the Garden during the exhibition match. Even if security had been tightened somewhat following the incident with Clara, it was difficult to imagine that other students would be denied entry at all costs.

But Kuroe continued in a soft voice, "Please listen calmly. Hollow Ark…is the only all-girls school for mages."

"Huh…?" Mushiki said with a grimace.

"From the teachers to the students to the administrative staff, the school is made up entirely of women. I can't speak for the grounds of the Fuyajoh residence, but at least when it comes to the academy itself, men are not permitted to enter."

"Th-that's…" Mushiki clenched his fists.

"In that case, I'll—" Hizumi said.

"Yes, that may indeed be possible. However, and I don't mean to sound harsh in saying this, even if you go to the Ark, I don't think you will be able to accomplish much, Hizumi. Your opponents will be the Fuyajoh family, experts in the field of magic. In all likelihood, they will refuse to meet with you."

"Th-then what should we…?" Hizumi's voice trailed off.

But Kuroe was no doubt right in that regard.

Mushiki caught his breath, then slammed his fists on his desk in frustration.

"What *are* we supposed to do, then? Are you saying we should just sit back and watch while she gets married off against her will?"

"…"

Kuroe, deep in thought, fell silent for a long time.

At last, she seemed to make up her mind.

"No… A delicate matter such as this needs to be entrusted to the right person."

"The right person…?" Mushiki said, then his eyes widened in comprehension.

"Indeed," Kuroe continued. "Someone they won't be able to refuse entry to, someone who can negotiate directly with Headmistress Fuyajoh, and—should worst come to worst—fight her way through the entirety of the Fuyajoh family."

"But someone who can do all that…" Hizumi frowned.

Mushiki, however, nodded along with newfound confidence.

"There's only one person who fits the bill."

"…!"

The moment that Mushiki set foot in the Engineering Room on the third floor of the Garden's central administration building, the technicians gathered there all turned his way, their breath catching in their throats.

But that wasn't an unreasonable response. After all, right now, Mushiki was—

"Please excuse the interruption."

Yes, he was currently Saika Kuozaki, the Garden's headmistress.

After that last discussion, Mushiki left the classroom, received a magical power-up kiss from Kuroe in a separate empty room, and returned as Saika.

"Ah, please continue. Don't mind me," he urged the technicians, who had stopped working, to rise to their feet and bow.

They looked a little perplexed by Saika's appearance but quietly did as instructed.

"M-Madam Witch? What can we do for you...?"

Yet there was one staff member who called out nervously, no doubt thinking that it wouldn't do to leave the visiting headmistress unattended.

"Ah, I heard that Hilde was here," Mushiki answered.

"The head of the technical department? She's in the seat farthest in the back—"

"Mm, thank you," he responded brusquely, before making his way to the far end of the room, Kuroe at his side.

The space was filled with various unfamiliar machines, like something out of a science fiction movie. Here and there, however, were old-fashioned magic tools with spells engraved on them, and strange creatures preserved in formalin, giving the room an overall chaotic feel. Unsure what function any of the items served, Mushiki stepped around them carefully to avoid touching them by mistake.

Finally, he arrived at an area carefully partitioned off from the rest of the room.

"..."

There, Hildegarde sat hunched over in a chair, staring intently at an arrangement of monitors laid out in a semicircle, muttering something under her breath.

"Hilde," Mushiki called out, tapping her on the shoulder.

"...Eeep! Yes?!" she squeaked, only now noticing the presence of her visitor. "Ah..."

She pulled her fingers out from the special console covering her hand, adjusted her misaligned glasses with her free hand, and glanced up to look at Mushiki's face.

She appeared somewhat frightened, but upon laying eyes on Mushiki—or rather, Saika—she seemed to relax a little.

"Wh-what's up...? I wasn't expecting to see you, Li'l Saika."

"Li'l Saika...?" Mushiki found himself repeating.

Kuroe had told him earlier that although Hildegarde was shy, she had a strong attachment to both Saika and Ruri...but he never would have expected her to use such a cute nickname. What a sweet sound. An instant number one on the list of names he wanted to recite out loud.

"Lady Saika." Kuroe prodded him from behind, bringing him back to reality.

He cleared his throat before continuing, "Ah, sorry for interrupting while you're busy at work. I have a favor to ask you."

"A-a favor...?" Hildegarde's eyes widened. "Li'l Saika is asking *me* for a favor...? Tee-hee... I—I see..."

She broke into a vaguely taut smile. At first glance, it looked like she was trying to force herself to smile—but in reality, she *was* genuinely pleased to be able to help Saika but simply wasn't used to being expressive.

"Mm, yes...all right. What should I do? Break into a bank's internal network and fiddle with the account balances? Replace the Cabinet Office's homepage with a naughty website? Pull the addresses of unfaithful cheaters and send them life-size statues of giraffes with payment on delivery. Or maybe—"

"Hilde," he said to stop her.

Hildegarde, having become suddenly talkative, flinched and fell silent.

"Don't tell me you're really doing those of kind of things, are you?"

"...N-no...?" She looked away, sweat beading on her forehead.

Mushiki could have sworn she had answered *yes* to it all, but maybe he was just imagining things.

"Well, anyway...Kuroe?"

"Yes. Take a look at this."

She handed the memory card from earlier to Hildegarde.

"...?"

Hildegarde looked at it curiously, then inserted it into the slot on her computer.

The next moment, Ruri's video appeared on the screen.

"...! Is this...?"

Hildegarde's eyes opened wide in astonishment as she looked to Mushiki with a grim expression.

"H-how strange... She didn't have anything to say to Lil' Saika...!"

"Yes, precisely." Mushiki nodded.

"Indeed," Kuroe added in a low voice.

"Putting what she's saying aside for a moment... Knight Hildegarde, what do you think? As head of the Garden's technical department, do you find anything suspicious about this video?"

"Hmm..."

Hildegarde narrowed her eyes as she watched the video once more, then made a few adjustments on her computer.

"...I can't give you an exact answer until I look a little more deeply... but it doesn't seem to be a composite or a fake... Hmm...I guess it's the real Ruri talking... Maybe...?"

"...I see."

Mushiki broke into a slight frown at this response.

If the video wasn't a fake, then there was a strong possibility that Ruri was being compelled to say all that in some way.

His face clouded over, and Hildegarde frowned, looking worried. "Wh-what happened...? It doesn't seem like Ruri to say all that..."

"No, it doesn't. The favor I wanted to ask you is related to this."

"O-oh. And what is it...?" Hildegarde asked, her head slightly tilted.

"I'm thinking of paying a visit to the Ark. I'd like you to lend me a hand," Mushiki said, running a hand through his hair.

Hildegarde responded with a forceful nod. "Y-yes...! Then I'll arrange for a bunch of giraffe statues...!" she answered with clenched fists.

"That's not what I meant," Mushiki cut in awkwardly.

◇

Two days had passed since Ruri's video was delivered to the Garden.

Riding in the back seat of a luxury car, Mushiki gazed out the window at the passing scenery.

Saika Kuozaki's lustrous profile was reflected in the beautifully polished glass window. He knew that if he allowed himself to start savoring it, he would stare at it forever, and so he tried his best to ignore it as much as possible.

Incidentally, he wasn't dressed in the Garden's uniform but rather a simple, well-tailored monotone dress.

The reason was simple—he was enroute to give a special lecture at another mage-training institute, so it wouldn't do for him to be wearing his usual uniform.

"Thank you, Kuroe. You're always looking out for me," he murmured as he turned to the figure sitting beside him.

"It was no trouble at all," a beautiful chime-like voice resounded in his ear. "In fact, it couldn't have been smoother getting permission for you to enter the Ark."

"Really?"

"Yes... When Saika Kuozaki of the Garden offers to give a special lecture, there isn't a mage alive who would refuse."

"Hmm. Huh."

At Kuroe's response, Mushiki could feel his face relax. Indeed, that certainly seemed to be the case.

"Just so you're aware, I tried to register you as a temporary exchange student at first, but the individual responsible for transfers at the Ark almost collapsed in a fit of laughter at the thought, so we made you a special lecturer."

Mushiki could only imagine how they must have felt. Surprised, no doubt.

"Well, that aside, it *was* a sudden request," he said with a shrug. "I'm sorry for all the trouble."

This matter was between the Fuyajoh family and Mushiki, but Saika was getting caught in the middle. It was with that in mind that he offered his apologies.

Kuroe, however, responded with a casual nod. "Don't worry. This is part and parcel of an attendant's responsibilities. Besides, Ruri is *my* classmate, too," she said.

"Kuroe…"

Mushiki stared at her profile, the corners of his eyes twitching with the beginning of a smile.

Her expression remained the same as ever. But her words, so unlike her usual self, filled his heart with emotion.

"Are you saying…you respect her?"

"Lady Saika," Kuroe responded more forcefully. "We will soon be setting foot in a different mage-training institute. Please choose your words carefully."

"…Hmm. I understand."

Inside, his heart was pounding, but he managed to reply with a relaxed smile.

The back seat was partitioned so that the driver wouldn't be able to overhear their conversation without using the intercom, but their expressions and gestures remained visible in the rearview mirror. On top of that, the driver was an employee of the Garden. It certainly wouldn't do for Saika Kuozaki to be seen being reprimanded by her attendant.

"By the way," Mushiki murmured to change the subject as he glanced out the window. "I've been wondering this for a while now, but where exactly *is* the Ark?"

It had already been close to an hour since they had left the Garden, the scenery outside having changed from residential areas and buildings to abundant nature.

Come to think of it, while the materials that Kuroe had prepared prior to his meeting with the other headmasters and headmistresses had included overviews of the other schools, the report on the Ark hadn't listed an address.

Kuroe likewise turned to look at the passing scenery. "We will be arriving shortly."

"Hmm…?"

Mushiki tilted his head in curiosity.

It was hard to believe that another one of Japan's five mage-training schools could be located just an hour's drive from the Garden. At the very least, he would have expected it to be in another region, like the other three were.

Perhaps sensing his unvoiced question, Kuroe spoke in a quiet voice: "We are extremely fortunate, Lady Saika. The Ark only comes this close to the Garden two or three times a year."

"…?"

Mushiki blinked in confusion when the car came to a stop. The driver, stepping out from the front seat, moved to open the back door.

"We have arrived, Madam Witch. Please," he said with a reverent bow.

"Ah, thank you."

To be honest, his head was still filled with questions, but he couldn't afford to let them show. And so, with exceedingly elegant movements, he alighted from the vehicle.

"Hmm," he murmured.

Spreading out before him was a field of blue.

The strong scent of the sea hit his nose. Sunlight gleamed on the surface of the water. Waves sounded intermittently, and the cries of the seagulls tickled his eardrums.

Yes… He was standing before the sea.

Strictly speaking, it wasn't a beautiful sandy beach like you might see in a promotional photo of a tourist spot, but rather a corner of a deserted wharf. It looked more like the kind of place where workers might unload cargo from a ship, or where mafia groups might engage in backroom deals. Certainly not the kind of beach where you might find families in bathing suits.

"This way, Lady Saika," Kuroe urged, having stepped out of the car first, a pair of tote bags in her hands.

He didn't like forcing her to carry his luggage, but it couldn't be helped if they were to show a typical relationship between a lady and her attendant. And so, deciding that he would thank her later, he followed a couple of steps behind.

She was proceeding toward a dock protruding out into the sea, though there was no sign of a ship at anchor. It was a dead end with nothing more than water ahead of them.

Yet—

"Is this…?" Mushiki murmured.

A strange sensation passed through his body as he approached the end of the wharf.

It was similar to what he had felt when entering the Garden—he was passing through a barrier, magic designed to conceal something from the outside.

By the time he recognized it for what it was—

A small boat had appeared before his eyes.

To be precise, he wasn't quite sure whether *boat* was the right word. It was a strange vessel, with a vague capsule-like design. But the way it floated in the water had him reaching for the closest word in his vocabulary.

Then—

"Saika Kuozaki, headmistress of Void's Garden. We've been expecting you."

Mushiki turned to face the voice that had suddenly called out to him.

Standing at the end of the wharf was a strange-looking figure—a young woman in a white sailor suit and a cloak resembling a haori. Her epaulettes and realizing device indicated that she was a mage. When had she appeared there? She must have been dispatched from the Ark.

As for her facial expression—Mushiki couldn't read it.

That wasn't to say that the figure was impersonal, lacking in individuality. But her face was hidden behind a fox mask with a curious pattern engraved on it.

He was startled for a moment, but it was common enough for mages to dress oddly—and above all, Saika Kuozaki wouldn't have allowed herself to be taken aback by this.

"I will serve as your guide during your stay with us," she said with a tranquil voice. "Please call me Asagi."

"Thank you for your hospitality."

"That's quite all right. As a member of the Ark, I'm honored to have been selected to greet the famous Witch of Resplendent Color. Please, come this way," the woman said, holding out her hand to guide them onto the *boat*.

Mushiki assumed this meant that they would be entering the vessel, and so nodding his head, he climbed aboard, Kuroe following a step behind him.

Even from inside, the *boat* was strangely built. A smooth and rounded transparent outer wall surrounded the seats, reminding Mushiki of an imaginary spaceship that he had once seen in a picture book.

"Let's proceed. Please be careful. It may get a little bumpy," Asagi said as she sat down at the pilot's seat and reached for the touch-panel console.

Then, with a low-pitched whirr, various parts of the *boat* were infused with a faint glow of magical energy.

The next moment—

"…!"

Mushiki's breath caught in his throat.

The *boat* sank down into the water.

"…"

Taken aback by this development, he turned to Kuroe. She, however, remained composed, only giving her head the smallest of shakes.

Apparently, this was no accident. They must have boarded a submarine… In a way, then, Mushiki wasn't entirely wrong when he thought it resembled a spaceship.

The vessel proceeded farther down for a full ten minutes.

"—."

Mushiki's eyes widened in surprise as he spotted something up ahead.

But that was only natural. Anyone would have shared his reaction on seeing *it* for the first time.

After all, *it* was a huge city resting at the bottom of the sea.

"That's…," Mushiki began.

"Hollow Ark," Kuroe whispered in a subdued voice so that the masked girl wouldn't overhear. "As the name implies, it's a mobile fortress city circumnavigating the oceans."

"Ah..."

After disembarking in the Ark, Mushiki let out a sigh both of admiration and of amazement at the sight spreading out before him.

He was staring at a circular city with a magnificent chalky keep at its center. The streets were laid out as if by design—as indeed they were—running in orderly rows with buildings of various sizes lining the long avenues.

A thick dome of air covered the mass of buildings, as though they were inside a giant goldfish bowl placed upside down on the seabed.

Looking up, Mushiki could spot countless schools of fish swimming under the shimmering sun, appearing as if they were flying in the sky.

It was a fantastic, unreal sight.

If the dragon's palace from the tale of Urashima Taro had been a real place, it must certainly have looked something like this.

"...Lady Saika." Kuroe called out his name.

"Hmm...? Ah," Mushiki answered, turning his gaze back ahead.

Right. He couldn't go around acting like a fresh-faced tourist while in Saika's body.

Then, as though waiting for him to come back to his senses, Asagi offered him a polite bow. "Allow me to take you to see the headmistress. Your luggage will be delivered to your accommodations, so please leave your bags here."

"I see. Lead the way," Mushiki said, following along with Kuroe.

They made their way down a sequence of beautifully paved roads toward the keep-like school building in the center of the city.

Along the way, he spotted countless students in the Ark's white sailor uniform. Come to think of it, Ruri had been wearing the same kind of outfit in the video that they had received.

Consistent with what he had heard about the Ark being an all-girls school, he spotted only women... The thought that he was making use of Saika's body to intrude upon this sanctuary of the opposite sex left him feeling like he was up to no good.

At that moment—

"Huh...?"

Mushiki's eyes twitched as one girl, wearing a mask and cloak atop her school uniform, stood out from all the rest.

"That mask and cloak..."

While the pattern on the mask was ever so slightly different, it remained remarkably similar to the one worn by the girl leading Mushiki and Kuroe.

"Yes," Asagi said in response to his unfinished question. "We are the Azures, the Ark's disciplinary committee. Our primary duties are to maintain security and public morals here at the Ark, but we're also, well, jacks-of-all-trades, you might say. If you need anything during your stay, please don't hesitate to tell one of us."

"Hmm..."

It seemed that their guide's mask and cloak weren't her own unique clothing style but were, rather, part of a uniform. No doubt each school had its own special characteristics in that regard. Mushiki nodded in understanding as they continued on their way.

A few minutes into their tour of this underwater aquarium, they arrived at the top floor of the school building enshrined in the center of the city—at the headmistress's office.

"Ma'am. I've brought Saika Kuozaki," the masked girl said.

With that, the double doors slowly swung open.

The girl remained by the door in a state of awe.

Likewise, Kuroe took a step back as though to say that she would wait here.

"..."

From this point on, the discussion would be between the heads of the two schools.

But Saika Kuozaki wouldn't lose her head in this situation, so Mushiki stepped inside, doing his best not to let his apprehension show.

Inside, the space was set out like an audience room, the design similar to the fortresslike building's exterior. At the back of the room was a raised platform, with a bamboo blind sectioning it off from the lower area. It was completely different from Saika's office, which was filled with countless shelves of books.

"Heh-heh, welcome. It's been a long time, Saika. I almost died of loneliness, not seeing you for a full week," said Ao Fuyajoh, the headmistress of the Ark, from behind the blind.

"Apologies," Mushiki responded with a gentle smile. "It took me a good amount of time to find the right tea leaves that'll match your standards."

"Oh dear." Ao smiled in amusement.

On the surface, they had exchanged friendly greetings with a touch of humor.

But Mushiki could feel the tension in the room—it was so strong that it made his chest hurt.

This wasn't his first conversation with Ao; they had met before at a conference consisting of the principals from each mage-training institute—as like-minded allies, so to speak.

Now, however, he had been forced to set foot in the Ark—her territory—to retrieve Ruri, whom they were unable to contact.

He would be more than happy if they could come to an amicable solution. But seeing as it was Ao who had decided on Ruri's marriage, the possibility of a hostile reception was far from zero.

Ao, too, was no doubt aware of all this.

Kuroe had described her as far from stupid. She was the kind of woman who wouldn't feel the slightest discomfort at a sudden visit from Saika.

But Mushiki still lacked sufficient information. He had been warned not to say anything until they knew what was really going on here.

Then again, another way of phrasing all this was that they wouldn't hesitate to take appropriate measures once everything was revealed.

"So what's with the sudden offer about giving a special lecture? The girl who received your request got quite the surprise."

"Not at all. I think opportunities for our schools to exchange ideas are invaluable."

"Even though you rejected my previous request?"

"...Ha-ha-ha... Did I?"

This was the first he had heard of it. He gave an empty smile to conceal his surprise.

"In this state of emergency, it's vital for all mage-training institutes to join hands. Wouldn't you say?"

"Well, let's leave it at that. Irrespective of your reasons, I welcome the offer. It isn't every day we have an opportunity like this." With that, Ao snapped her folding fan shut. "Say, Saika?"

"Yes?"

"The resurrection of the Mythologia, the Ouroboros...is a serious situation, no? Moreover, its whereabouts remain unknown. It might be mass-producing Immortals even as we speak."

"...Yes, that's right."

"During such a critical time as this, no mage would be foolish enough to poke her nose into the affairs of another's family and home out of mere curiosity. No?" Ao asked, lowering her voice.

"—."

Mushiki's chest tightened at these words, which were so at odds with the lighthearted greeting they had exchanged a moment ago.

But Saika Kuozaki wouldn't let this fluster her. So Mushiki spread open his hands, taking on a generous tone to conceal his distress. "Of course not... Clara Tokishima has turned on our people. I'm vindictive at heart, as you know. I will repay her in full; you can be sure of that."

"Oh my... How stalwart of you. But I guess that's how you've always been. It's frightening at times... I wouldn't want you as my enemy."

"Ha-ha. Rest easy. There's no way we could end up as enemies, is there? Not unless you hurt any of my beloved students," he said, his tone carrying a hint of menace.

"Oh? Indeed," Ao said with a faint smile. "On that point, you can rest assured. I would never seek to do such a thing... But know this, Saika. It seems that the Azures are a little on edge, given the previous

incident. I know you have no intention of doing so, but you would be doing me a great favor if you refrained from any actions that could invite misunderstanding."

"Oh, there's no harm in being cautious. How dependable of them. By all means, allow them to fulfill their duties... And you needn't worry on my behalf. I won't be at all concerned if the kittens want to play."

"Even kittens have claws. Do be careful. I wouldn't want to see a dear friend get hurt."

"Hmm."

"Oh-ho-ho."

After this exchange of words, the two traded small smiles.

Though they both maintained a friendly tone, the tension in the room was palpable. A weak-minded observer would have found it hard to watch.

Nonetheless, Ao had no intention of continuing their conversation indefinitely, waving her hand as though to change the topic. "Well, it might be a difficult time, but this is still a rare opportunity. Do enjoy yourself a little. It's been a quite a while since your last visit, yes?"

"...Hmm. I think I will," Mushiki responded as he left the headmistress's office.

As soon as he stepped outside, the doors swung shut behind him.

Then, with perfect timing, Asagi, who had been waiting outside, bowed. "Allow me to show you to your rooms. This way, please."

"Thank you," Mushiki said with a slight nod, following her down the corridor with Kuroe by his side.

"Kuroe?" he whispered so that Asagi wouldn't hear.

"Yes?"

She nodded along to his summary of the discussion, as though she already knew everything that had happened inside. Given that they were dealing with *her*, she had probably guessed the meeting's contents—though it wasn't out of the realm of possibility that she had actually listened in somehow.

"...As expected, Ao is aware of the true purpose of our visit."

"Yes...she must be," Mushiki said.

Kuroe nodded. "But it doesn't seem like she intends on going out of her way to stir things up so long as we don't make it explicit... In any event, we need to locate Ruri first. Is she being restrained or held in confinement? Is she being permitted a degree of freedom under supervision? Is she presently able to act on her own volition? Without knowing any of this, we won't be able to plan our next moves."

"...Ah." Mushiki nodded as he clenched his fists.

"...Yes?"

At that moment, Asagi, who had been walking along ahead of them, turned around with suspicion.

Apparently, his voice had grown louder without his meaning to.

"It's nothing," he said with a shake of his head. It's just been so long since I last visited. You have a wonderful school here."

"I'm honored. I'm sure the headmistress will be pleased to hear that," the girl said calmly as she led Mushiki and Kuroe out from the school building and into the dormitory area.

The day's classes, it seemed, were already over, with girls in white uniforms gathering to chat in small groups at the various commercial establishments that lined the streets.

Some of them noticed their visitors, watching with piqued curiosity as they passed through.

"Hey, hey, who's that being led around by the Azure?"

"She's so beautiful... A visitor from the outside, I suppose?"

"I feel like I've seen her somewhere..."

"Huh? Doesn't she look like Madam Witch from Void's Garden...?"

"Seriously? Wow..."

And so rumors began to spread like wildfire.

Come to think of it, Kuroe had said something about the Ark having few visitors, seeing how it was a mobile city constantly roaming the sea. The people here probably didn't have many opportunities to interact with those from other mage schools. Perhaps it was a rare thing for a guest to visit.

"Hmm..."

Saika could hardly ignore their gazes as she walked past them, and so Mushiki gave a smile and a small wave at the groups of girls staring at him, prompting a flurry of squeals and blushes.

Then—

"...Lady Saika." Kuroe caught her breath, before giving his sleeve a slight tug.

Given how well she normally kept her emotions under control, this was rare, and Mushiki couldn't help stopping in wonder.

"Hmm? Ah, sorry. I guess I'm going a little overboard smiling to all the students here..."

"What are you talking about? Take a look at *that*."

"Huh...?"

He cast his gaze in the direction she was pointing—and fell suddenly silent.

The reason was simple. There could be no failing to recognize the girl across the street.

Her long hair was tied up in twintails, and her eyes showed unshakable willpower.

She was wearing the Ark's white sailor uniform, but there could be no mistaking her...

It was his sister, Ruri Fuyajoh, whom they had been unable to reach for more than a week now.

"..."

There she was, making her way down the street surrounded by several girls.

Perhaps because of her status as a scion of the Fuyajoh family, she seemed to be incredibly popular. The girls around her were all smiling happily as they tended to her needs.

But even in the midst of all these girls, Ruri's eyes were lifeless, and her expression was dark and morose—as though she couldn't even hear the voices of those around her.

Mushiki had never seen her like that at the Garden, and his chest tightened.

"..."

They were fortunate to have located her so quickly, but something was clearly amiss. He took a deep breath as he called out to her, "Ruri—"

Yet—

"Headmistress Kuozaki. Please don't shout in the school district."

At that moment, Asagi, as though sensing what he was about to do, positioned herself in front of him.

No, that wasn't all. Appearing practically out of thin air, others dressed just like her—the Azures—rushed to separate him and Ruri.

"What...?"

Mushiki furrowed his brow, but quickly regained his composure as he gracefully brushed his fingers through his hair.

"Oh, dear me, I apologize," he said. "Yes, it certainly won't do to make a ruckus on school grounds."

"Thank you for your understanding."

Asagi gave a bow, and the other Azures followed suit—they were so in sync, they could have all been following the exact same programming.

"But," Mushiki continued, "isn't that a slight exaggeration? I just happened to see an old acquaintance and thought I should call out to her. It would be beneath the dignity of the Ark to stand in the way of something so trivial."

"..." Asagi listened in silence, but it wasn't long before a muffled voice sounded from behind her mask: "Headmistress Kuozaki. Please consider your influence and standing. You are the most powerful mage in the world. Even the smallest of gestures when coming from someone as highly respected as you could have a profound effect on those watching... Furthermore, you have been invited to the Ark to give a special lecture. I would like to ask that you refrain from showing favoritism to any one student in particular."

"...I see, I see..."

Mushiki let out an impatient sigh at this roundabout excuse.

"What a quaint thing to say. Don't I have every right to speak to a beloved student of mine?"

"Beloved student? Who in the world are you talking about...? If you mean Ruri Fuyajoh, who was formerly enrolled at the Garden, I believe she has already informed you of her intent to withdraw from your school."

"...Oh?" Mushiki narrowed his eyes in irritation—when Kuroe tapped him on the shoulder, urging him to calm down.

Glancing back down the street, he saw that Ruri's group had already left.

...Right, it wouldn't be a good idea to stir things up here and now. With that in mind, he gave Kuroe a slight nod as he let out a sigh.

"...I'm a little tired. Can you show me to my accommodations?"

"As you will," the masked girl answered with a polite bow.

"Well now..."

After arriving at his assigned room, Mushiki let out a long sigh as he took in his surroundings.

He had been given a room in the guest quarters at the back of the dormitory building—the Ark's best, no doubt. It was decorated with luxurious furnishings and was a little too spacious for one person.

"What do we do now?" Mushiki muttered, in no mood to feel excited by all this.

After leading him and Kuroe here, Asagi had handed them her contact information and told them to reach out to her if they needed anything before promptly disappearing. Right now, it was just the two of them.

Of course, another room had been prepared for Kuroe, but they had met in Saika's room to discuss their next moves.

"Please wait a moment," Kuroe said with one hand raised as she narrowed her eyes. Then, concentrating, she intoned, "First Substantiation: Eye of Inquiry."

A ringlike pattern unfurled around her neck, her eyes lighting up.

Mushiki had seen this technique before. As he recalled, it was a form of analytical magic that allowed her to see though the structure and composition of other objects.

With her eyes aglow, Kuroe cast her gaze around the room. Finally, giving him a quick nod, she deactivated her world crest.

"That was?"

"I was concerned about privacy, so I checked just in case."

"...I see." Mushiki felt his eyes twitching at Kuroe's words.

It was clear by now that Ao doubted their intentions for coming here. He should have anticipated this.

"However, Ao isn't a fool. She will have expected us to check for anyone listening in. She won't go out of her way to look for our weaknesses. This was merely a precaution." Then, after a short pause, she added, "Let's consider our plans moving forward."

With those words, she pulled a small cell phone and a pair of wireless earphones from her pocket, handing one to Mushiki.

After fitting it into his ear, he could make out a small voice: "...A-ah... Testing, testing... What was it again...? Whew..."

It was Hildegarde. Her voice was a little hard to make out, but that seemed to be a volume issue on her end, not a connection one.

"Um...can you hear me? Li'l Saika? Li'l Kuroe...?"

"Yes, no problems here."

"Ha-ha... This is like playing spy, huh...?"

"It kind of is, isn't it?" Mushiki responded with a soft smile.

Hildegarde must have been pleased to hear that he shared her opinion, as she gave a soft *"Tee-hee-hee..."*

"More importantly, Knight Hildegarde, what is the current situation?" Kuroe asked brusquely, holding the other earphone to her ear.

"Ah...y-yes...," Hildegarde responded, flustered. *"You have the device I gave you before you left, yes? I was able to use it to access the Ark's internal network. If you give me enough time, I think I can break through their security. Just be careful that the battery doesn't run out...,"* she added in a hurry.

Indeed. This was what Mushiki and Kuroe had asked of her before leaving the Garden.

To confirm Ruri's current location, gather information on the Fuyajoh family, and counter any security measures at the Ark that might stand in their way in the event of an emergency.

For those reasons, they had asked her to hack into the Ark's network.

...It was hardly a noble approach, and Mushiki was a little worried that it skewed too close to how Clara had attacked the Garden, but they had to be prepared for any eventuality.

"The Ark, by its very nature, has its own campus-wide network, which limits how much can be accessed from the outside... With a physical connection to the main server, you might have a shot, but it'd still be pretty difficult... However, with this neat little gadget, once you're in, you can do just about anything... Tee-hee-hee. Did they honestly think they could keep me out with such weak security...?" Hildegarde seemed to be talking to herself, gasping in realization after saying all that. "A-anyway... leave it to me. I'll let you know when there's progress." With that, she hung up.

Mushiki and Kuroe, each wearing a single earphone in one ear, exchanged glances and brief nods.

"Let's see what Hilde can come up with...and think about what *we* can do, too," he suggested.

"Yes," Kuroe answered.

Of course, it wasn't going to be that easy. And so, crossing his arms as he got to thinking, he added, "We were lucky to find Ruri on the first day...but the situation doesn't look good."

"No. She isn't being confined...but she wasn't acting like her usual self, either."

"Ah..." Mushiki frowned, recalling how she had looked when they'd spotted her.

While he had seen her only from a distance, she certainly hadn't seemed like her usual self. *Brainwashing, manipulation*—words that he would have otherwise considered poor jokes flashed through his mind.

All the same, pessimism would get them nowhere. With a shake of his head to clear his negative thoughts, he continued, "There's no point worrying about that now. First things first, let's think of a way to reach out to her."

"My thoughts exactly. The main issue will be the disciplinary committee—the Azures," Kuroe said, resting a hand on her chin.

"Yeah," Mushiki said with an exaggerated shrug. "I wasn't expecting them to interfere so blatantly like that."

"But the fact that they did is proof that they don't want Lady Saika interacting with her. If they believed there was no harm in letting you see her, they wouldn't have taken this approach."

"I see…" Mushiki nodded in understanding.

Certainly, if they had completely brainwashed her, it was hard to believe they would be so overly sensitive. Their overzealous approach in guarding her was a weakness that could potentially be leveraged.

"But how *can* we contact her? Given the situation, she must be under surveillance. If posssible, I'd like to avoid getting into a big fight…"

"There *is* another way," Kuroe said with a confident nod. "One where it wouldn't be unusual for you and Ruri to meet at close range. It would also be difficult for the Azures to interfere."

"Oh? What is it?" Mushiki asked.

"Lady Saika," Kuroe answered softly, "Please fulfill your original purpose in coming here."

Chapter 3
Unlocking the Heart
⇜ of a Princess Held Captive ⇝

Even among mage-training institutions, each school had its own unique characteristics that were influenced by their location.

Hollow Ark, which journeyed through the world's oceans, often dealt with annihilation factors that arose in the sea. For this reason, the layout of the school's training grounds was quite different to those at the Garden.

The fields consisted of sand, and they even went so far as to replicate the ebb and flow of the waves. Seawater had eroded a portion of the dome of air surrounding the Ark, giving the training area the appearance of a beach or bathing area.

And now, at that very training ground—

"Um, this *is* the right place, isn't it?"

"Yes. This is where it said to go on WeSPER."

"I knew it! It *was* Madam Witch I saw yesterday!"

Several excited students had gathered.

Looking closely, Mushiki also spotted the occasional older mage—teachers, no doubt. In fact, the area was laid out almost like an event venue.

But that was understandable.

After all, today was the day of Saika Kuozaki's special guest lecture.

"It seems like a big hit," he observed, peeking out the window of the small building set aside as a waiting room at the corner of the beach.

"Indeed," Kuroe answered. "It's rare that one has the opportunity to see a mage on the level of a school principal give a live demonstration. Even more so when they visit from outside one's own campus. And especially when it's you, Lady Saika. It's only natural that you're the center of attention."

Well, Saika Kuozaki was renowned as the headmistress of Void's Garden and the world's strongest mage. With her past achievements, she was literally a living legend. It would be hard to find a mage who hadn't heard her name.

That being said, the crowd was smaller than Mushiki had expected...

Only a limited number of students had been selected to attend.

Given that a mage of her caliber had gone to the trouble of visiting the Ark to give a special lecture, it would only have been natural for any and all aspiring mages to want to participate.

That said, here they were.

To top things off, there was something else bothering him.

"By the way, Kuroe," he began.

"Yes?"

"What's with this outfit?" he asked, staring down at himself.

He was presently wearing a sporty halter bikini.

The tight swimsuit hugged Saika's proportions perfectly. Her body was truly a work of art. In fact, Saika's figure was so beautiful that Mushiki had hardly been able to bring himself to move away from the mirror since changing into the bikini.

It wasn't just Mushiki who wore a swimsuit. Kuroe and the other girls gathered in the training grounds were all dressed similarly, though their swimsuits were of different designs. Combined with the location, it had the air of a seaside school rather than a special lecture.

Kuroe, however, remained composed. "Even at the Garden, we change into sportswear when we use the training arenas, do we not?" she asked pointedly.

"Ah, right. Yeah."

"Precisely."

"Talk about huge regional differences, though," Mushiki said, overcome with a strange feeling.

Kuroe tilted her head. "You don't like it?"

"No, I think it's wonderful. In fact, I'd like to introduce this kind of thing at the Garden."

"People will make a fuss if you were to lose your mind, Lady Saika. Please refrain from doing anything rash," Kuroe said flatly.

Mushiki nodded. That *would* cause a commotion.

"Anyway, I get it… I was just a little surprised. The design isn't bad. Yours looks good, too, Kuroe."

"Thank you," she replied. She sounded nonchalant, but something about her response suggested that she wasn't entirely indifferent.

At that moment, there was a knock on the door to the waiting room.

"Come in," Mushiki said—and with that, a young woman stepped inside.

She was wearing a mask and cloak over her uniform, clearly marking her as an Azure. From the pattern on the mask, Mushiki recognized her as Asagi from yesterday.

"Excuse me…Headmistress Kuozaki. Explain all this," she demanded in a disapproving tone.

Mushiki couldn't read her expression because of the mask, but he could sense that she had on a deep frown.

"Explain what? There was no specified format for my lecture, so I decided to give a practical class. Here, we can gather more students than in a classroom or auditorium, wouldn't you agree…? Is there a problem?"

"…" Asagi fell silent.

Yes, this was the plan that Kuroe had suggested yesterday.

The Ark was working to prevent contact between him and Ruri, but so long as Saika was visiting the school as a special lecturer, they couldn't stop him from teaching the students. If he was ever going to have a chance to reach Ruri, this was going to be it.

If it was held in a classroom or auditorium, there was a high possibility that Ruri would be kept away, ostensibly for lack of seating.

For that reason, they decided to do a practical lesson open to all, with no limit to the number of students permitted to attend.

They had made sure to broadcast the event beforehand, and Mushiki had asked Hildegarde to announce the class on WeSPER, a social networking website used exclusively by mages.

There was little in the way of entertainment at the Ark, and as more than ninety percent of all mages were said to have an account on WeSPER, it would only be a matter of time before everyone at the school learned of the lecture.

Even if Ruri's cell phone had been taken away from her, it would be practically impossible to keep her out of the loop once word spread to every corner of the school.

"...This is only a class. Please refrain from conversing any more than necessary," Asagi said bitterly.

"Oh, I understand," Mushiki responded with an exaggerated nod. "Let's get started, Kuroe."

"Understood."

With that, Mushiki exited the waiting room and went straight to the white sandy beach.

"...Ah! Look, everyone! There she is!" bellowed the first student to notice Saika, pointing excitedly his way.

Then, like a crashing wave, the other girls let out a roar of cheers.

"Is that Madam Witch?! From the Garden?!"

"She's even more beautiful than I imagined!"

"Ah, she just looked this way!"

And so on, each voice more animated than the last.

Though overwhelmed for a moment by the attention, Mushiki didn't feel at all bad that Saika was proving to be so popular. He fixed the audience with a relaxed smile and waved in their direction.

"*Kyaaarrrggghhh!*" the girls cried out at the top of their lungs—as if he was a celebrity.

The next moment—

"—."

Mushiki's eyebrows twitched slightly.

Behind the girls, he had spotted Ruri.

He and Kuroe exchanged glances for a moment, along with the slightest of nods.

"...Looks like we've cleared the first hurdle," he whispered.

"Yes," Kuroe murmured. "But I don't think we can afford to be too optimistic."

She was right, of course. It was clear as day that Ruri wasn't in a sound state of mind.

"Indeed. If she was her usual self, she'd be up there in the front row, camera at the ready, crying out, *Ah, Madam Witch! You're so gorgeous! You're like a brilliant, glittering star! So radiant, I can't even sleep at night!* And she'd be taking photos nonstop."

"That's a very specific example."

"I can't even begin to guess how she's managing to stand there so calmly."

"Perhaps you're imagining things. One might say she's being more decorous now than she usually is."

The two of them proceeded across the beach while talking, soon reaching the front of the crowd.

Then, after waiting for everyone's enthusiasm to subside, he introduced himself in a clear and calm voice, "Greetings, everyone. I'm Saika Kuozaki, headmistress of Void's Garden. As fortune would have it, I'm joining you today here at the Ark as a special lecturer. We'll only be together for a short while, but I look forward to showing you some new tricks."

Like that, the students burst into excitement all over again, the swimsuit-clad girls throwing out their chests as they jumped for joy.

It was an incredibly stimulating sight. If Mushiki had been his usual self, he might have averted his gaze so as not to risk getting too excited and increasing the amount of magical energy leaking from his body.

However—

"…Hmm."

His lips twisted into a dauntless grin.

The reason was simple. He had already witnessed a stronger weapon of mass destruction—Saika in a swimsuit—in the waiting room mirror a few minutes ago, so he had become somewhat immune to the sight of other girls (incidentally, it had been necessary for him to take two power-up kisses from Kuroe as well).

"Now then," he continued with a relaxed expression, "let's begin with warm-up exercises. Could you form pairs of two?"

"*Yes!*"

The students were quick and eager to respond to his instructions, forming pairs with their friends.

The area around Ruri erupted with an explosion of noise.

"Lady Ruri, if you don't mind, won't you partner with me?!"

"No, no, with me!"

"No, no, no, no, choose *me*!"

It seemed that the students were bickering over who would be paired with her. Yet even in the midst of all this, Ruri maintained an expressionless doll-like look, responding only with a noncommittal "Hmm…"

But Mushiki had already anticipated this development after witnessing how those hangers-on had acted around her the day before.

"Oh dear, it looks like you can't decide on a partner. Then there's no helping it," he said with a soft smile as he approached the group. Then, pointing toward Ruri, he said, "You—I suppose you'll have to pair up with me."

Perhaps it was just his imagination, but he sensed that Ruri's facial muscles twitched slightly in response.

"Headmistress Kuozaki!" sounded a voice from behind him—Asagi.

He had also expected this.

"What is it?" he asked, glancing back with an exaggerated look over his shoulder. "Surely a member of the disciplinary committee wouldn't interfere with a *class*?" he said, emphasizing the final word.

"…Ngh," Asagi grunted in frustration. Though clearly unhappy with this development, she said nothing more.

Mushiki turned back to Ruri and extended his hand. "How about it? You don't want to?"

"...No...that's not it... I would be honored...," she answered with a blank expression and a faltering voice.

The next moment, the other students burst out in excitement.

"Lady Ruri and Madam Witch together...?!"

"I-is this demonstration really free to watch...?!"

"It's like how sea urchin and wagyu beef are even more delicious when eaten together...!"

There didn't seem to be any further objections, and so with a soft smile, Mushiki took Ruri's hand and returned to his original spot.

"Now then, let's get started. Be thorough. Lack of proper preparation can risk serious injury."

"*Yes, Madam Witch!*" The students cried back in cheerful voices.

If anything, the cohort here at the Ark seemed to be even more motivated than that at the Garden. The students were all on the tips of their toes to see Saika's first live demonstration. Mushiki understood how they felt. Even he wanted to take this class.

But right now, he had other priorities.

After a simple stretch to warm up, he had Ruri sit down on the beach, then positioned himself behind her and pushed slightly on her back so that she would lean over.

Then, so that Asagi wouldn't be able to see, he positioned his lips close to her ear and whispered, "I was worried about you, Ruri. I'm glad you're safe."

"...!"

She remained expressionless, but her body noticeably twitched.

Something was indeed wrong with her. But it was certain that she was also reacting to his words. And so, without letting Asagi catch on, he continued in a whisper, "Are you being watched? Blink once for yes, twice for no."

"..." Gritting her teeth, Ruri's eyes snapped shut once.

"Do you truly want to remain here at the Ark?"

"..." Two blinks.

"Are there surveillance cameras monitoring you where you're staying?"

"..." One blink.

"Is there a way to contact you in secret?"

"..." Two blinks.

Like that, he continued to ask her a few more questions.

Though her answers were somewhat strange, she was able to respond to his every query. It was like she was unable to freely control her body, as though every effort required a surge of willpower.

"...Hmm..."

Was it possible that Ao had hypnotized her, but she was now slowly regaining her sense of self through contact with her idol, Saika...?

It wasn't unthinkable... And in that case, he might be able to completely undo the hypnosis with stronger stimuli.

It took Mushiki only a moment to come to this decision—and with that, he immediately began to take action.

"Try to lean in a little further, Ruri," he said, pressing close against her back and pushing down with his weight.

Then, his lips almost grazing her earlobes, he whispered, "It isn't good to hold back... Give it your all... Unburden yourself..."

"...Gah... Grrrhyuuu..."

A mysterious noise sounded from somewhere deep inside Ruri's body as she leaned forward as far she could go. She was incredibly flexible, her legs almost parallel with her torso.

Her face, Mushiki realized, had turned bright red. He realized he had pushed down on her back harder than he should have.

"Oops."

As he eased up, Ruri's bones creaked, and steam was coming out of her ears.

"Sorry," he murmured. "Was I a little too strong?"

"...N-no...," Ruri answered like a rusty robot.

Her expression remained vacant, but that was unmistakably an audible response.

He would have to press further.

"Everyone," he called out, glancing back at the students. "Have you all finished doing your warm-up exercises? Kuroe, shall we move on?"

"Yes," she answered with a brief nod as she retrieved a small bottle from the basket that she had prepared in advance. "Very well. Everyone, please apply this mermaid lotion to your body. It is a protective liquid imbued with magic. It will protect you from immense water pressure in the unlikely event of an accident underwater. It's difficult to apply by oneself, so please work in pairs and be sure to help your partner." With those words, she began handing out the vials to the various groups.

Mushiki likewise took a vial from Kuroe, opened the lid, and turned back to Ruri as he poured the viscous liquid onto one hand.

"Come on, Ruri. I'll apply the lotion for you," he whispered with an innocent smile.

"...Kee... Kyupee..." Again, Ruri's expression remained unchanging, but an eerie sound escaped from the depths of her throat.

Paying that no heed, Mushiki circled around her and began to apply the lotion onto her skin, poking at her shoulders, arms, and back with his fingers.

"...Very good, Ruri. Like this... Yes, a little more...," he whispered into her ear as he traced the contours of her back.

"Oh... Ngh... Mm..." Ruri trembled, as though something was trying to break free from her body.

"Hmm... Maybe that will do it?" Mushiki said with a satisfied sigh after painstakingly rubbing the lotion into her skin.

Ruri was his sister after all, so he could hardly bring himself to apply the cream all over. Besides, if he slipped up, he could end up reverting back to his original form. This was as far as he could go.

"Now, Ruri. Can you apply it on my back?"

"...Eeep?!"

Ruri's breath caught in her throat, and she turned her head a full 180 degrees.

Seeing how they had paired up, this should have been part of the natural flow of the class—but for Ruri, it seemed to be a huge deal.

…Well, he could understand how she felt. It might have been through the power of lotion, but she was basically granted permission to touch Saika's back. Of course, the psychological impact would be immeasurable.

But that was his goal.

Knowing Ruri, who considered herself Saika Kuozaki's (unofficial) promotion manager, this shock might well be enough to free her from whatever spell she was under.

"Then I'm in your hands," Mushiki said, giving her the bottle of lotion and turning his back to her.

Then, with a slow, delicate movement, he gathered his silky hair to one side and exposed his skin.

"Ah… Ah… Ah…"

Ruri, her body quivering almost like a zombie, squeezed the lotion onto her hand and carefully reached for his back.

Then, just as her fingers grazed his skin—

"Aaarrrggghhh?!"

As though her brain had been struck by lightning, she cried out in sudden agony and fell flat to the ground.

"Kyargh?!"

"L-Lady Ruri?!"

"Did something happen?!"

All at once, the students around them cried out in shock. Asagi, observing from the rear, fell down to her haunches as if about to set off in a sprint.

But despite everyone's reactions—

"Huh…?!"

Ruri's eyes shot open, and she leaped into the air with all the momentum of a spring-loaded toy.

"Wh-what…am I…?"

Then, blinking, she looked around.

Her voice, actions, and facial expressions were at last those of the Ruri that Mushiki knew so well.

It looked like she was finally back to normal. Though he was filled with joy and relief, it would be out of character for Saika to clench her fists in triumph in front of so many onlookers, so he made do with a composed smile.

"Hey, Ruri. Good morning. How are you feeling?"

"…! Madam Witch…!" Ruri spun around, immediately kneeling before him. "I'm sorry for missing classes without permission!"

"Oh? Don't worry about that," Mushiki answered, glancing at Asagi. "Let's save the discussion for later. We're still in the middle of a class."

"…Ah."

His gaze and words seemed to be enough for her to grasp what he was hinting at.

Mushiki nodded in satisfaction, then turned back to Ruri. "Then can you rub more lotion onto my back, please?"

"Ah… Ah…"

The next moment, Ruri, despite having come back to her senses, grumbled again in that monotonous voice.

Perhaps sensing the situation, Kuroe darted over and vigorously slapped the lotion onto Mushiki's back herself.

"Please refrain from complicating the situation any further," she said flatly.

"Now then…"

Once Ruri had calmed down, Mushiki resumed the class.

While he had achieved his first goal of making contact with Ruri, with Saika Kuozaki officially at the Ark as a guest instructor, he couldn't afford to put in a half-hearted effort here.

"Then let's begin… Right, you there," he said, pointing to a nearby student, who immediately tensed up. "Ha-ha, don't be so nervous… What do you usually use here at the Ark when fighting in water or under the sea?"

"U-um…you mean an aerial device?" she stammered, reaching for the object that resembled a choker at the base of her neck.

An aerial device was a fourth-generation magical tool used to create a thin layer of air around one's body to enable breathing and movement both underwater and in a vacuum. Until just yesterday, Mushiki had never heard of it, but Kuroe had been kind enough to fill him in.

"Yes. Those are indeed what we use most of the time. But battles can happen at any moment. It isn't always possible to enter one fully prepared, and there's always the potential for an accident. It's only because this is a training session that we have the luxury of applying lotions to protect ourselves from increased pressure... So I would like to share with you a trick to use in case of an emergency, for when you're unable to make use of any of these items," Mushiki announced in a clear, easy-to-understand voice as he lifted a finger into the air.

He had to speak confidently here to prevent tarnishing Saika's public image, so he found himself reciting the words that Kuroe had taught him the night before.

According to Kuroe, students at the Ark conducted regular training when it came to their substantiation techniques. As such, if the school was going to go to the trouble of bringing in a guest lecturer, it would have to be to develop knowledge that wasn't normally available here.

His current ruse was simply a means for them to infiltrate the Ark, but Saika wasn't the type to cut corners, irrespective of the circumstances. She was pretty cool in that respect, at least as far as Mushiki was concerned.

"Kuroe," he called out.

"Yes," she answered, taking a step forward. "I will now take over for Lady Saika to demonstrate," she said to the students.

Everyone's gazes turned to Kuroe.

She remained perfectly calm, without the slightest hint of nervousness. Then, narrowing her eyes, she murmured the words "...Pneumatic field, range deployment, 170-70-60..."

"What was that...?"

"An *invocation*, right? See, that's the formula you use for a second substantiation. We did that in class."

"Ah, now that you mention it..."

As they watched, a small commotion broke out among the students.

Having captured everyone's attention, Kuroe ran to the outer edge of the Ark—toward the open sea.

And just like that, she dived straight into the wall of air that separated the school from the water outside.

The wall of air shook for a moment. Then, Kuroe was thrown out into the depths of the sea.

The bubble of air encompassing the Ark wasn't so weak that it could normally be breached by a human, but it seemed that the area near the training grounds had been adjusted somewhat to allow for deep-sea combat exercises... No wonder. That was why the area was designed like a beach, and why their gym uniforms resembled swimsuits.

"Huh...?!"

"She went out into the open sea without even using a device?!"

"She's got no oxygen, and even with that lotion, the water pressure..."

The students' eyes widened in astonishment, but Kuroe remained unperturbed, floating in the water outside.

If they looked closely, they would have seen that a thin barrier of air had formed around Kuroe's body. Mushiki hadn't noticed it while she was still within the Ark, but now that she was outside, he could clearly make it out.

After floating in one spot for a short while, then swimming in a few small circles, Kuroe made her way back to Mushiki and the others.

Her hair and body, incidentally, remained perfectly dry.

"So how did you find it?" she asked, sending the dumbfounded students into a round of applause.

"What *was* that...?"

"Is that what you meant by activating magic with an invocation?"

"Yes," Kuroe said in response to the students' questions. "Using this three-measure formula, we can create a simple barrier around the body to retain oxygen. Of course, it isn't as accurate or as effective as an aerial device, but it can still be used for several minutes. There are various techniques that enable you to breathe and act underwater, but the most efficient, I believe, is to find the right balance between deployment time and duration of effect. Techniques like this aren't used so often now that we have fourth-generation magical devices, and fifth-generation substantiation techniques have also become more common. But those all require considerable expertise to manufacture or maintain. Compared to magical tools that require specialized equipment and knowledge, and substantiation techniques that can differ in effectiveness based on the abilities of the individual using them, one could argue that these simpler methods have the advantage of being highly versatile. On top of that, it's a simple process to customize the composition of such spells. You might even say that there's something akin to poetry in adjusting the parameters so as not to hinder efficiency while at the same time cutting down on the words required as much as possible…" Having unusually delivered everything so quickly, Kuroe seemed to realize that the audience was watching, speechless, and she paused to clear her throat. "…Or so Lady Saika tells me."

"Ah…yep." Mushiki nodded along.

She was acting like she had been forced to add that last part, but in any case, it was indeed *Saika* who'd said it.

Though she usually played the role of a cool and collected attendant, it seemed that once she started talking about her interests, there could be no stopping her. To think that Mushiki had been able to witness this other side of her all because they had come to the Ark… He couldn't stop his body from shaking as he turned his mind to Kuroe's potential.

"Now, seeing as we're all here, let's give it a try. First of all—"

At that moment, Mushiki fell silent.

The reason was simple—all throughout the dome-shaped pocket of air that encompassed the Ark, a shrill warning alarm had begun to sound.

"…!"

"This is…!"

Fear was written all over the students' faces.

Mushiki knew that sound. Even at the Garden, it rang out from time to time.

It meant—

"…An annihilation factor," he murmured.

"It seems so." Kuroe nodded.

The next moment, a gigantic flowerlike *thing* appeared in the sky—no, in the *sea*—overhead, its petals spreading out to grip the dome of air that surrounded the Ark.

The force being applied from the outside and the air pressure contained within the Ark fought against each other, unleashing a deafening roar.

"Kyargh?!"

"Wh-what *is* that?!"

All at once, the students began to cry out in dismay.

"…!"

It was only then that Mushiki finally recognized it for what it was—appearing in the sky over the Ark was a swarm of tentacles spread out in a radial pattern, each consisting of hundreds of suction caps.

"That's—"

"Annihilation Factor No. 302: Kraken. Among the annihilation factors that appear in the sea, it isn't particularly uncommon. However, it's rare to see one this large. If we don't act soon, it may well prove dangerous," Kuroe explained in a matter-of-fact tone.

This sounded like it could be a critical situation, but Mushiki couldn't sense even the slightest hint of worry from her.

Then, a girl—Ruri—ran up to the two of them.

"Madam Witch!" she called out.

"Ah, Ruri. That's quite a large kraken, isn't it?" he answered, repeating what he had just learned from Kuroe. "Let's deal with it before it damages the Ark."

Ruri nodded. "Yes. But you don't need to do anything, Madam Witch. I'll—"

"No, that won't be necessary," a voice interrupted, prompting Ruri to look back in wide-eyed shock.

Mushiki turned around to find Asagi nearby.

"Asagi—"

"Problems at sea are the Ark's specialty. Please leave this to us," she said, lifting her right hand into the air to issue a command. "Begin."

With that, a series of torpedo-like objects were suddenly launched from the Ark's outer edge.

No, they weren't torpedoes… Straining his eyes, Mushiki realized that they were all girls, and they were dressed like Asagi.

There were no fewer than thirty of them in total.

Enveloped in air pockets generated by their aerial devices, the girls left long trails behind them as they shot through the sea like meteors cutting across the night sky.

"…Ready," Asagi began.

With that order, in a single, undisturbed movement, the deployed Azures surrounded the giant kraken and raised their right hands in front of them.

The next moment, double-layered patterns appeared above their heads, while glittering javelins materialized in their hands.

"…Shoot," Asagi commanded as she swung her hand downward.

With perfect timing, the Azures all cast their second manifestation weapons straight at their target, and countless spears of light pierced the kraken from all directions.

The giant annihilation factor's tentacles writhed in agony, but it wasn't long before the creature ceased moving and was gradually swept away by the ocean currents.

"Phew…"

Mushiki could only look on, wide-eyed. The whole affair had taken only a few brief seconds.

"…Remarkable. I've never seen such perfect teamwork," Kuroe commented.

"I'm honored by your praise," Asagi said with a polite bow.

Then, turning back to them, her line of sight obscured behind her mask, she continued, "Ruri's body is incredibly important in the lead-up to her wedding. We cannot permit anyone or anything to harm her… We members of the disciplinary committee are determined to protect her from any and all threats."

"…"

Mushiki's eyebrows twitched at that declaration.

But that was to be expected. Asagi seemed to be suggesting that no matter what he or anyone else might try, they would never permit Ruri to leave the Ark.

But the very next moment—

"…!"

A sound like the rumbling of the earth rang out, violently shaking the Ark.

"Wh-what the…?! I thought we just destroyed the annihilation factor…?!" Asagi caught her breath.

"Captain!" called out another Azure, running up to her.

"What's going on?"

"Below us! There's another kraken on the seabed…!"

"What…?!"

Just as Asagi voiced her alarm, several huge shadows swayed around the outer edge of the Ark, the violent sound of the earth splitting growing louder and louder.

Something—a being as huge as a towering skyscraper—was climbing out from under the sea floor and enveloping the Ark.

Only after the Ark was completely surrounded did everyone realize that those apparent *tentacles* were simply too gigantic.

"I-impossible… It's too big…!" Asagi exclaimed, her voice tinged with dismay.

But that reaction was understandable. After all, this annihilation factor was an order of magnitude more massive than the previous kraken had been.

On top of that, ten of its tentacles were now gripping the Ark like a child holding a small ball in the palm of their hand. If it tightened its hold any further, the entire Ark might collapse in on itself.

"Notice to all disciplinary committee members within the Ark! Request assistance from the headmistress before—"

"No, that won't be necessary," Mushiki interrupted calmly as he gave the panicking Asagi a gentle tap on the shoulder.

"…! Headmistress Kuozaki!"

The annihilation factor was unmistakably a threat, and if left unchecked, the whole Ark could very well be destroyed. Should that happen, the countless students who lived here would be mercilessly cast into the depths of the sea.

Yet Mushiki's expression betrayed neither panic nor dismay.

After all—

The world's most powerful mage was on the scene.

"This is the perfect opportunity for a live demonstration. Everyone, watch carefully... Saika Kuozaki is here," Mushiki said with a calm smile as he launched himself from the beach and soared high into the sky.

A student himself, he was still inexperienced as a mage—but he was now inhabiting Saika's body, and without question, she was the strongest in the entire world.

"—."

Mushiki passed through the wall of air encompassing the Ark and leaped out into the sea—and at the same time, a four-layered world crest unfurled above his head.

"The creation of all things. Heaven and earth alike reside in the palm of my hand."

It almost looked like a witch's hat, shining in resplendent color.

Mushiki looked down at the scene below him—at the tentacles of the giant kraken gripping the Ark—and slowly raised a hand before him.

"Pledge obedience... For I will make you my bride."

At that moment—

The world was transformed.

That was no metaphor or joke. The undersea landscape beneath him became distorted, morphing into something completely different.

Saika Kuozaki's fourth substantiation—the pinnacle of manifestation techniques, and the ultimate goal of many modern mages.

It was the most potent of all techniques, capable of rewriting the world around oneself.

Now they were contained within a red-hot cave filled with boiling lava—the lower reaches of a cauldron of hell, where the air, if breathed in, would scorch one's lungs black. An environment as harsh as this would inevitably reject all living things.

And the annihilation factor was cast out into this realm of extremes. The creature behind those tentacles proved to be some form of colossal mollusk, so massive that it could probably consume a whale whole.

Mushiki slowly flipped his hand over, clenching his fist tightly.

With that, the world around him condensed in a rapid spiral—quickly crushing the kraken to death.

"Hmm..."

He loosened his grip and exhaled deeply, as though to blow away gunpowder smoke from a fired gun.

With that, the scenery reverted to normal.

He returned to the Ark and flashed everyone a beaming smile.

"...!"

The students, left stunned by the spectacle that had just taken place, seemed to finally grasp that it was all over, erupting into a wave of cheers comprising equal parts awe and envy. Mushiki gave them all an exaggerated nod as he waved in their general direction.

"That was brilliant, Lady Saika," Kuroe congratulated him.

"Ah," he replied as he approached Asagi, still standing where he had left her.

Then, as though to throw her words back at her, he declared with an unfaltering smile, "We may belong to different institutions, but we are all allies... I share the same desire to protect Ruri at all costs."

Asagi stared back at him as she clenched her fists. "I see."

She uttered the words quietly, her tone gentle—but her overall attitude was harsh.

And so Mushiki and Asagi faced off against each other behind their masks, both showing the other an undaunted grin.

That night, after finishing dinner, Mushiki and Kuroe found themselves in Saika's room on the top floor of the guest house.

With them both being treated as guests of honor, the food was top-notch, and the room was luxurious as could be. On top of that, a member of the Azures would rush to their side should they ever need anything. If they had been here just for sightseeing, Mushiki wouldn't have had a single complaint.

"...Well then. What now?" he asked.

"Indeed," Kuroe replied.

As the two exchanged words, it was hard to describe their expressions as particularly friendly.

In the end, the class had been canceled partway through to deal with the aftermath of the annihilation factor attack and to inspect the damage to the Ark. As a result, they had been separated from Ruri.

While Mushiki had succeeded in making contact with her through an act of deception, Asagi and the others would no doubt be more vigilant the next time around. Whether the same strategy would work again remained to be seen.

That being the case, their only option was to pray that their plan would prove to be a success. Mushiki sat back to take a sip of the black tea that Kuroe had brewed for him, and he let out a deep sigh.

At that moment—

"...!"

His eyebrow twitched as a gentle knock sounded from behind the door.

"It's open. Come in," he said.

With that, the door slowly swung open as a girl stepped into the room. Before he knew it, Mushiki had risen from his chair.

"Ruri..."

Yes. Standing before them was Ruri, dressed in loungewear and a pair of sandals.

"Thank goodness," he said with a relieved sigh. "So you *did* get my message."

"Y-yes...! There's no way *I* wouldn't understand Madam Witch!" Ruri exclaimed, clenching her fists in excitement.

As it happened, Mushiki had been carefully conveying messages to her by tracing letters on her back with his finger.

That they were staying in this room. The way here. And that they had asked Hildegarde to disable the surveillance cameras along the route.

It was a dangerous bridge, that was certain, but Ruri appeared to have made it across without issue.

Seeing her doing well, Kuroe let out a relieved sigh. "It seems that she's no longer under the influence of any hypnotic suggestion."

"Hypnotic suggestion? What do you mean?" Ruri, however, tilted her head as though she didn't quite understand.

"…? Didn't Ao place you under hypnosis or something similar? When we saw you yesterday, you looked so empty and emotionless that we almost mistook you for someone else," Kuroe pointed out.

"Ah…" Ruri exhaled. "About that… I mean, I hadn't been able to see Madam Witch since leaving the Garden. And they took my smartphone away, so I couldn't go over any pictures, video, or even audio… It's like I've been fasting for a whole week. I was completely frazzled."

"…You're using her as sustenance?"

"More like oxygen to breathe, I guess?"

"Oh? So you died of suffocation, you're saying?" Kuroe responded nonchalantly, tilting her head. "Then why were you acting so strangely in class today?"

"I mean, Madam Witch? In a bathing suit? Without any advance warning…? It was a feast for the eyes, but there's no way you can just go and stuff yourself with chateaubriand steak after a week of fasting… You need to start off with rice gruel or something…"

"Rice gruel."

"Right… Like admiring dot art with a Madam Witch motif or sniffing a handkerchief from the store at the Garden. You need to start off with something simple like that."

"Wouldn't a photograph of Lady Saika or a personal handkerchief be enough?"

"Th-that'd be too strong! Like seasoned rice! You can't eat that on an empty stomach!" Ruri cried with a squeal, her cheeks turning red.

"…Then why did you seem to come back to your senses when Lady Saika touched your body?" Kuroe asked.

"I guess it must have been like a forced shutdown? After a mental overload? I mean, it *did* help clear my head."

"I see." Mushiki nodded in understanding.

"..." Kuroe continued to ponder this explanation, eventually giving up. "Is that so? Does that mean this *wasn't* you?" she inquired, pulling her smartphone from her pocket, and playing a now-familiar video—the one Ruri had sent to the Garden.

"Huh...?" Ruri stared blankly at the screen, her eyes opening wide. "What the...?! I don't remember saying anything like that! Or filming anything, either!" she exclaimed in a hoarse and indignant voice.

Mushiki let out a weak sigh. "So it *was* a fake?"

"It sounds like it," Kuroe said. "The fact that Knight Hildegarde couldn't determine as much suggests it wasn't made through image manipulation."

As the two spoke, Ruri's shoulders slumped in apparent realization. "This was sent to the Garden...? S-so the reason you're here, Madam Witch...?"

"Yes. I didn't believe it was real, either... I came to ascertain my lovely student's true wishes. You can hardly expect me to stand idly by when presented with something this absurd, no?" Mushiki answered with a wink.

Ruri covered her mouth, tears welling up in her eyes, deeply touched by his words. "F-for me...?! *Sniff*... I'm honored...!"

The next moment, she fell to the ground with immense force, prostrating herself before him.

Kuroe, perhaps wanting to move the conversation along, cleared her throat. "Anyway, we now know your true intentions, Ruri. Next, we need to formulate a concrete plan moving forward—a way to end this talk of an engagement and bring you back to the Garden."

"Yes, that's right. But that's just the problem. What are you thinking of?" Mushiki asked.

Kuroe brought a hand to her chin as she sank deep into thought. "I have an idea. But there's one issue."

"Hmm...? What is it?"

"First of all..."

And so she began to briefly explain her strategy.

Mushiki nodded along in agreement, while Ruri likewise gave her assent, blushing slightly.

"Interesting. It's certainly worth a try," Mushiki said.

"B-but, Madam Witch. Who at the Ark would do something like that...?" Ruri asked hesitantly.

"I can think of one person," Mushiki answered confidently. "Can you leave this to me?"

◇

The next day, in the headmistress's office in the Ark's central school building—

"...Hmm?"

After a long pause, Ao Fuyajoh tilted her head in an exaggerated display of doubt. "Would you mind saying that again?" she intoned from behind the bamboo blind.

Her voice was calm and collected, betraying no hint of discomfort or anger. In fact, she might not even have been actively trying to intimidate her visitor.

All the same, Ruri couldn't help feeling like she was fighting against an immense force of pressure as her every word rang out.

That was little wonder. Just a short distance in front of her was the head of the Fuyajoh family, a woman who no doubt ranked among the five most powerful mages in the whole world.

"..."

Yet she couldn't back down. Clenching her fists to steel herself against the tremendous weight that seemed to be pushing down on her from above, she continued, "Yes. As I said, I can't accept this marriage proposal."

Ao sighed. "Oh? You came all this way just to say that? I thought you had already said as much after you came back to us?"

"That's...," Ruri groaned, raising her eyebrows in alarm.

It was certainly true that she had declined the marriage offer immediately after boarding the Ark. Of course, Ao hadn't been in much of a mind to listen and had dismissed her protests. Ruri was by no means happy with how the last exchange had ended.

But Ao must have thought the discussion was over, as she continued as though addressing a stubborn child: "Don't be selfish, Ruri. As a mage, you must understand that you have a responsibility to pass the power within your bloodline on to the next generation, yes?"

"That's... I realize that. I'm not saying I'll never get married or have children! But I'm still young, and I don't want to marry someone I don't even know—"

"You're the most talented young woman in the Fuyajoh clan. This may sound harsh, but your body doesn't belong to you alone. As a Fuyajoh, as a woman, I ask that you listen to me... Besides, I've chosen the best possible mage as your suitor. I'm sure you'll approve... Or is there some other reason why you can't get married?"

"...!"

Ruri's eyebrow twitched at this last question.

But this was her only chance. Determined, she bowed.

Fighting to quiet her racing heart, she said aloud the words that she had prepared earlier: "Yes...I've actually already decided who I want to marry."

"...Hmm?" Ao asked doubtfully. "Are you saying you already have a lover; someone you've committed your heart to?"

"Ah...yes..."

Ruri blushed at the word *lover*, but she forced herself to answer clearly.

Ao tilted her head askance as though summing her up. "...Just so we're clear, who exactly are you talking about?"

Ruri had been expecting this question. And so, clearing her throat, she answered, "Actually...he's here now."

"Huh?" Ao's voice rose slightly.

This last response had evidently come as a surprise.

But Ruri's only option was to press on before the family head could regain her composure. So without pausing, she called out to the door behind her, "Come inside!"

The door to the headmistress's office swung open, and a young man entered the room.

He had light hair. Kind eyes. A neutral countenance.

Walking nervously over to Ruri's side, he offered Ao a polite bow.

"Nice to meet you, Headmistress Fuyajoh... I'm Ruri's boyfriend, Mushiki Kuga."

"...Gah?!"

Though she should have been ready for this, Ruri couldn't help coughing violently as if spitting up blood, her face turning bright red.

Back to the previous night—

"...Wh-wh-wh-wh-wh-wh-wh-wh-what?!"

In Saika's guest room, Ruri's hands trembled in anxiety, and her voice quivered.

"What are *you* doing here?!" she snapped at the top of her lungs, pointing straight at him.

But that was an entirely natural response.

After all, standing before her was Mushiki, back in his original body.

Yes. After stepping out from the room just now with Kuroe, he had undergone a quick transformation before coming back inside.

"Um...well, how should I put it?" he began, at a loss on how to answer.

"He came from the Garden with us, of course," Kuroe said, throwing him a lifeline.

It wasn't a lie. He nodded his head in awkward agreement.

"Right, right. I was worried about you, Ruri. But I'm glad to see you're safe."

"Wh-what...? Don't say embarrassing things like that!" she blushed, averting her gaze.

A few seconds later, she took a deep breath to calm her nerves. While still looking away, she continued, "...Sorry for making you worry. I thought I'd be home by now, too."

"This isn't your fault."

"...Right. My family is always so old-fashioned, and I know this is all on them. But for Madam Witch to come all the way out here for the likes of me..." At that moment, her eyebrow twitched in sudden realization. "Huh? Where did she go? Didn't she step out with you just now, Kuroe?"

"..."

"..."

Both Mushiki and Kuroe fell silent, not sure how to respond—and that unnatural silence only made Ruri shake all the stronger.

"Wh-what gives, you two? Did I say something weird...?"

"...No. Lady Saika had something to see to, so she's stepped outside for a short while," Kuroe answered.

"Really...? Then shouldn't we go somewhere else?" Ruri said in a panic, preparing to leave the room.

Mushiki and Kuroe both had to place themselves in her path to stop her.

"It's okay," Mushiki said. "She gave us permission to stay here."

"Indeed. She urged us to continue the strategy meeting," Kuroe added.

"R-really...?"

Looking uneasy, Ruri stopped in place—but she quickly shrugged and turned back to Kuroe. "Hold on. We were talking strategy earlier. Don't tell me Madam Witch was talking about Mushiki?!" she cried out loud, her cheeks turning bright red.

But that wasn't an unreasonable response. After all—

"Yes. As I mentioned earlier, bigamy is prohibited even for mages," Kuroe answered calmly. "If you already have a lover to whom you have pledged your future, would that not change the attitude of this other prospective suitor?"

Ruri's face continued to grow redder. "B-b-b-b-b-but why *Mushiki*?!"

"On the contrary, is there anyone more qualified than him? This is the Ark, a world of women ruled by Headmistress Fuyajoh. I doubt we will find anyone else here willing to stand up against Ao, let alone any other men."

"B-but we're brother and sister?!"

"Hmm. So you can't get married?"

"That's not what I meant! Nghhh!" Ruri objected—more forceful this time, for some reason. "It's rare, but people from mage families do sometimes marry close relatives in order to maintain their bloodline! Genetic problems can be solved with magic so long as both parties are of roughly the same generation!"

"Huh? Wow. That's amazing," Mushiki stammered.

Ruri's face turned an even deeper shade of red. "Don't misunderstand me here! I'm just stating an objective fact!"

"Huh? Ah, yeah." He nodded.

Kuroe cleared her throat. "In other words, you're saying there will be no problem with it."

"Nghhh…!" Ruri groaned in frustration.

After all, she was the one who had provided a solid counterargument. She would hardly be able to protest now.

"B-but…wh-what about you, Mushiki?! Y-you… You're okay with it?" she asked, turning toward him.

Her gaze didn't have the same vigor as before—rather, it was more like she was timidly trying to size up his thoughts.

"I…," he began, casting his eyes to the floor as he pondered.

He already had someone he had devoted his heart to. Of course, there was no telling whether she would respond to his feelings for her, but he would be lying if he said he didn't have any qualms at the thought of pretending to be someone else's lover.

But…if this was what was required of him to save Ruri, that was a different story.

"Of course I'm okay with it," he answered, looking at Ruri with determination as he took her hand in his own. "By all means, let me play the part of your boyfriend."

"Huh…?! O-okay…"

Ruri's eyes shot open, and her eyes began to spin.

◇

And so we return to the present moment—with Mushiki standing beside Ruri, the mood slightly tense as he faced the ruler of this sea fortress.

Headmistress Ao Fuyajoh had been watching him in silence for quite some time now.

Though he was unable to read her expression behind the bamboo blind, he could sense that she was taken aback by this latest development.

But that was only to be expected.

After all, Ruri had suddenly brought someone she claimed to be her lover, to whom she had pledged her future.

"..."

Ao remained silent for a while longer, then finally moved her hands with a rustling sound.

The next moment, an alarm rang out from within the office.

"Huh?" Mushiki said, startled. The door slammed open, and several Azures members stormed in.

"You called, ma'am?"

"Yes. We have an intruder," she said in a ruthless tone.

Mushiki and Ruri stared back wide-eyed.

"Huh...what?!"

"Hold on! At least hear us out—"

But before Ruri could finish, Ao pointed her folding fan at Mushiki from behind her bamboo blind. "There are a great many things I want to say, but first thing's first—why is there a *boy* in the Ark? I don't recall giving him permission to enter."

"...Ah." A cold sweat broke out on Mushiki's forehead.

Right. He had been so preoccupied with the mission that he had forgotten that critical rule.

Next to him, Ruri pulled a face, as if she was just as surprised as Ao was.

"...Hold on, you didn't come here with Madam Witch...? Did you smuggle yourself in?" she murmured.

"No, um...I was worried about you, is all," Mushiki whispered.

"...Ugh..."

Ao sighed. "In any event, this issue comes first before any talk of lovers. See him out."

"*At once*," the Azures members said as one, closing in around him.

Ruri held out an arm to shield him. "Wait, please, Lady Ao! Mushiki was just trying to help me...!"

"That's none of my concern. I don't know how you managed to get in here, but—"

At that moment, Ao suddenly fell silent.

"Mushiki...?" she repeated dubiously, her eyes widening in surprise. "*Mushiki*, you said...? You don't mean Ai's boy, do you?"

Ai. That was indeed his mother's name.

"Y-yes... Do you know of me?" he asked.

"..."

Ao fell silent for a few moments as she pondered her next words. "...Well. It's an extremely rare thing, a male being born within the first degree of kinship from the main bloodline of the Fuyajoh clan."

"Really?" Mushiki asked, honestly surprised.

Ao stroked her chin suggestively. "Hmm... Yes. This boy... Yes..."

"...?"

At Ao's reaction, Mushiki tilted his head—but before he could say anything more, she swept her hand in an exaggerated gesture.

"Very well. Step aside," she said to the Azures.

"Are you sure, ma'am?"

"Yes. He may be a man, but he's related to the Fuyajoh clan. I will make a special exception and permit him to remain."

"...Very well."

With that, the Azures offered a polite bow before leaving the room.

And so once more, it was just the three of them occupying the now-silent office.

"Now then," Ao began from behind her bamboo blind. "If you're Ai's boy, that would make you Ruri's older brother, yes...? In other words, brother and sister have fallen in love?"

"Yes," Mushiki answered.

"Ngh," Ruri stammered, holding her hands to her chest, and twisting her body side to side.

"I promise to make her happy."

"Nghhh!"

"I love her, from the very bottom of my heart."

"Ugh! Ngh! Eeep!"

"So please, give us your permission to marry!"

"*Kwawdrftgyfujikolp!*"

Ruri, her face turning redder as Mushiki went on, finally let out a strange cry.

Ao tilted her head in consternation. "Ruri seems to be taking damage from hearing your words."

"She's always like this," Mushiki responded strongly.

"R-right…" Ao cleared her throat. Then, looking at Ruri, she asked another question: "Is this true, Ruri? This isn't just some ploy to get out of your betrothal?"

"Th-that's…" Ruri hesitated.

Well, Mushiki could understand how she must have felt. The situation being what it was, it couldn't be easy putting all this into words.

But they had to overcome this.

"Ruri." His gaze clear, he stared deep into her eyes.

"…!" She jerked back, her cheeks as red as ripe tomatoes. "Eeep! Y-yes… Ruri…I mean *I, me*…I—I…love…m-my…brother…," she stammered.

"Hmm…I see." Ao let out a long sigh, then pointed her fan back at Mushiki. "In that case, prove it."

"Prove it…?"

"Yes. Hmm, yes… How about you kiss each other—now?"

"—."

"Wh-what…?"

Both Mushiki and Ruri choked up at this latest remark.

Kuroe had applied a magic spell on him, so it was unlikely that Mushiki would inadvertently power up from a single kiss. At the very least, he was unlikely to transform into Saika from one.

But his heart remained true to her all the same. He would be lying if he said he was comfortable kissing another woman, even his sister.

"..."

But he had to get his feelings in order.

Then, the imaginary Saika who dwelled deep in his mind revealed herself. *"Why are you hesitating? With a single kiss, you can convince Ao Fuyajoh to give up on the marriage partner she's decided on. Was your resolve this weak?"* she asked, patting him on the shoulder.

With that faint shock (of the imagination), Mushiki made up his mind, gently grabbing Ruri by the shoulders and pulling her toward him.

"...! M-Mushiki...?"

"It's okay, Ruri. Leave it to me."

"...!"

Her body trembled, then she slowly closed her eyes... She, too, it seemed, had found her courage.

Mushiki brought his face close to hers, their lips so close now that they could feel each other's breath.

The next moment—

"...I—I—I *caaannn't!*"

With a bright red face, Ruri delivered a powerful uppercut to his jaw, and Mushiki crashed onto the floor.

◇

"...So it was no good."

"...It was no good."

Ruri and Mushiki, having returned to Saika's guestroom, both slouched in disappointment.

"It didn't work?" Kuroe asked in her usual indifferent tone after hearing their report.

"No...I thought we put on a good show, Ruri especially," Mushiki explained.

"...R-right..." Ruri averted her gaze, her cheeks turning pink as she thought back to it all.

"We need to devise a new plan," Kuroe began. "Can you tell me precisely what happened?"

"Right," Mushiki answered. "I said I loved Ruri from the bottom of my heart, and—"

"You don't need to repeat it verbatim! Nghhh!" Ruri screamed at the top of her lungs, throwing a nearby cushion at him.

After it hit him squarely in the face, Mushiki returned the cushion to the sofa and explained how things had transpired in the headmistress's office.

"...I see," Kuroe murmured, her hand under her chin as she pondered their next moves.

"I'm sorry... This is all my fault," Ruri, still blushing, said with a frown.

"Well, you could hardly have been more incompetent," Kuroe quipped.

"Nghhh..."

"Then again, even if you had kissed, Ao may well have made more increasingly unreasonable demands. Don't worry too much about it... From Ao's point of view, it wouldn't make sense to give up on a prospective marriage partner for a close relative... The Fuyajoh clan is a prestigious mage family, so the suitor must be of similarly high station. Of course, he must also have considerable skill as a mage."

"I see..." Mushiki frowned. "In other words, for anyone to be accepted as Ruri's lover and overturn this betrothal, they're going to have to be a powerful mage from a good family background?"

"There will be other conditions as well, of course, but that's it in essence... The problem is that such individuals are few and far between."

"Huh? I can think of someone, though. The perfect candidate," Mushiki said.

"...*Huh?*"

As he went on, Kuroe and Ruri exchanged shocked looks.

◇

"………Er, would you mind saying that again?"

Thirty minutes later, in her office in the Ark's central school building, Ao Fuyajoh was literally holding her head in her hands.

It wasn't hard to understand her reaction.

After all, setting foot now in her office was—

"Of course. I'll say it loud and clear… I, Saika Kuozaki, love Ruri Fuyajoh from the bottom of my heart… I ask for her hand in marriage."

It was none other than Saika Kuozaki, the Witch of Resplendent Color herself.

Of course, inside her body was the exact same person as before, but there was no way that Ao could have known that.

Yes. If it was Saika, no one could possibly complain about her family pedigree or magical ability. After all, she was the head of Void's Garden and lauded as the strongest mage in the world. It was no exaggeration to say that no one else on earth could hope to surpass her when it came to those two things.

Incidentally, Ruri was cowering beside him.

She didn't need to say the words out loud for Mushiki to hear them: *"W-wow, Madam Witch would do this for me…? I'm sorry, I'm so sorry… I don't deserve this… I'm so honored, I could burst into flames here…"*

"…Are you being serious, Saika?" Ao asked somberly, sighing heavily.

"Of course," Mushiki responded with a strong nod. "Ruri and I love one another… Isn't that right, Ruri?" he asked, hugging her around the shoulders.

"Eeep…! Yes!" Ruri, who was startled, opened her eyes as wide as could be.

"…C-can this…can this really be happening?" Ruri said under her breath, before murmuring what sounded like a litany of clichéd song lyrics: "Oh my goddess…? Is this real? Am I dreaming? A shooting star in a lapis lazuli sky…?"

Mushiki could understand how she must have felt. If he had been in her position, and Saika had offered to do the same for him, he would have responded no differently.

At that moment, Ao spoke as though just now remembering something: "But, Ruri, didn't you say you were in love with your brother?"

"...! Th-that's..." Ruri fell silent, the blood rushing to her cheeks.

But this was where Mushiki stepped in. "Let's not dwell on the past. Love always strikes without warning."

"...Speaking of which, where did that boy disappear off to? I may have given him special permission to stay here, but it won't do to have him wandering around campus."

"I have no idea what you're talking about."

"..." Ao fell silent, raising a hand to her head as if plagued by a headache. "...I have many questions," she began, before quieting down again for close to a minute.

"Go on," Mushiki pressed.

"...Saika, you're a woman," Ao pointed out, the critical matter that he had been waiting for.

Indeed. While none could surpass Saika in background or in ability, there was that one hurdle.

But of course, Mushiki hadn't come all this way unprepared. So, with a dauntless smile, he asked, "You won't accept a same-sex marriage? I don't want to have to put up with any anachronistic objections here."

"...I don't mean to deny such couples. But that does mean you two can't have children, no? Given that Ruri belongs to the Fuyajoh clan, that would be rather troubling."

"Hmm...," Mushiki answered, stroking his chin. "Ao?"

"What?"

"Do you know what induced pluripotent stem cells are?"

"Saika?!" she shouted forcefully.

Mushiki gave a slight shrug. "Well, we can come back to that later. Ruri may even have a change of heart down the road. Perhaps one day we'll separate, and she'll find someone else. The possibility is always there. People's hearts do change."

Mushiki himself was well aware of the sophistry of this argument.

In essence, he was suggesting that when Ruri becomes older and decides that she wants to find another marriage partner, Saika would step aside. But in that case, this certainly looked like a mere excuse to break off the marriage proposal that Ao had arranged.

But when it came from the mouth of Saika Kuozaki, even this contradictory suggestion carried an air of credibility.

Mushiki relaxed, fearlessly gazing at Ao. "So that's how it is. If some unscrupulous individual was to try to tear us apart, I don't know what I would do."

"…"

Ao fell silent once more at this declaration.

Then, after letting out a deep sigh, she glanced at Ruri. "Is it true, what Saika is saying, Ruri?"

"…Y-yes…! Fly me away to the Milky Way!" she said, saluting.

Though he couldn't understand the meaning of those words, Mushiki could see that she was signaling agreement.

Ao exhaled again, then pointed the tip of her fan toward him.

"…Then kiss each other and prove your love," she ordered, throwing out the same task that she had issued earlier.

"…"

"Hmm."

Ruri caught her breath, while Mushiki narrowed his eyes.

They had both been expecting this, and they were already prepared. There was no need to hesitate. Kuroe had likewise given them the go-ahead, telling them that this was an emergency, that there was no need for either to hesitate.

Right. In other words, there was no problem in them doing this.

"…Ruri. Come here," Mushiki whispered gently as he placed an arm around her shoulders.

"Eeep?!" Her voice trailed off, her face turning red all over again.

Mushiki pressed on, lifting her chin with one hand.

"M-M-M-M-M-Madam Witch…?"

"You don't want to?"

"Th-that's not it…!"

"Then leave this to me. It's okay. Don't you worry about anything," he said in a sweet voice, bringing his lips closer to hers.

But just before they could make contact—

"Ah..."

Faced with this unimaginable development, Ruri's brain must have overloaded, her consciousness flying off into the Milky Way.

"It didn't work."

"I'm so, *so* sorry!"

No sooner had they returned to Saika's room than Ruri leapt down and prostrated herself, apologizing vociferously. Her jumping height, flying distance, and kneeling posture were all first-class performances.

As if grasping everything just from this one brief exchange, Kuroe sighed. "It was no good?"

"No. Things went well during the first half, but then..." Mushiki explained what had happened.

"I see." Kuroe nodded.

Incidentally, Ruri had remained kneeling the whole time.

"If even Lady Saika couldn't change her mind, that must mean Ao has no intention of retracting her decision, no matter who the prospective partner is... Ruri, please look up. Even if you had succeeded, there is a strong possibility that she would have made further unreasonable demands."

"R-really...?" Ruri raised her face in trepidation.

"Yes, it's true," Kuroe continued. "Although it's also true that you gave a feckless performance."

"Uwaaaaaaaaa!" Ruri burst into tears at this last remark.

"Kuroe," Mushiki reprimanded her.

"Apologies. It was just a little funny, her reaction just now." Kuroe bent down to soothe the sobbing Ruri.

After a few moments, Ruri regained her composure.

With that, Kuroe rose back to her feet. "I *am* a little worried, though," she said.

"About what?"

"Ao. I remember her being more accommodating in the past."

"Hmm..."

Mushiki tilted his head, sinking deep into thought. Ao certainly hadn't seemed the accommodating sort from what he had seen—but he hadn't known her anywhere as long as Kuroe had. Perhaps something was amiss.

"So you're saying this talk of marriage has some deeper significance?" he asked.

"...Perhaps." Kuroe narrowed her eyes, having yet to figure out the answer. "In any event, let's continue this tomorrow. If we push too hard, Ao may well toughen her stance. There are still a few days left before the wedding ceremony. Let's take our time and come up with a better plan."

"Right... If I stay out too long, the Azures might catch on to us. I'll go back to my room for the rest of the day. They'll probably have figured out I'm working with you now that they've seen us together in front of the headmistress, Madam Witch, but there's no point giving them an excuse to crack down on me." Ruri turned to Mushiki and politely bowed. "Excuse me, Madam Witch. I'll drop by again tomorrow."

"Ah. There's still much to do. Get some rest."

"Yep!" Ruri answered cheerfully as she left the room.

"...Hmm."

In the office of the Ark's headmistress, Ao let out a small sigh in the hope of lifting her gloomy spirits.

She had had a great deal on her mind lately: from the revival of the Ouroboros to the weakening of the Tower.

There was also the appearance of two record-setting krakens at the same time. The Azures and Saika may have managed to save the day... but Ao, who had been defending the seas for longer, couldn't help having a bad presentiment.

Yet despite all that, her biggest concern was something else entirely.

"...I wouldn't have expected Saika to come here in person."

Saika Kuozaki—the world's most powerful mage. Never in her wildest dreams would Ao have expected her to try so blatantly to interfere in her plans for Ruri's future.

Even Ao, who wielded absolute power in the Ark, was at a disadvantage when it came to her. After all this time, she still regretted going along with Ruri's wishes and letting her attend the Garden. Then again, it was no doubt the Garden that had made her into her present self, but it pained her to have to admit that.

"...And Mushiki, too? What is *he* doing here?" she muttered bitterly, resting a hand against her head. "It's all falling apart..."

But at that moment, she stopped herself.

No. To be more precise, she was forced to stop because of a sudden cough.

"...Gah... Geh..."

She pressed a hand against her mouth to restrain the violent attack.

A few moments later—she pulled her hand away, her breathing ragged.

Reddish-black blood clung to her fingers.

"...I suppose we had better pick up the pace," she muttered in a chilling voice as she clutched her bloodstained hand.

Chapter 4
A Solemn Ceremony, a Vow amid Blue Flames

"Tea is ready, Lady Saika."

"Ah, thank you."

It was the day after the Fake Lover Operation. Mushiki took a sip from the cup of tea that Kuroe had prepared for him and let out warm breath in his top-floor guest quarters.

It was ten to five in the afternoon. Classes were finished, and the residential areas in the Ark were filled with girls in school uniforms.

An elegant moment, with dinner just around the corner.

But neither he nor Kuroe had time to take a break.

"She should be here soon, right?" Mushiki murmured.

"Yes. Perhaps it's taking a little longer for the students to disperse," Kuroe responded.

Ruri seemed to be particularly popular here at the Ark. For some reason, Mushiki found himself thinking about the throng of adorers milling around her and chuckledly softly.

He and Kuroe were presently waiting for Ruri to join them to plan their next moves.

"Only five days remain before the wedding ceremony. We must find some way to break off the engagement before then."

"Yes, indeed. But what exactly can we do…?" he asked.

Kuroe raised two fingers, as though making a peace sign. "We can discuss the details once Ruri arrives, but we have two options... The first is to direct our attacks at the groom."

"The groom...?"

"Yes. No matter how insistent Ao may be, if Ruri's marriage partner refuses, she will be forced to concede."

"I see. Interesting. In that case—"

But before he could finish, Mushiki tilted his head. "Hmm? Speaking of which... Just who *is* the groom?"

Right. He had been taken aback by the sudden announcement of Ruri's pending marriage, and even though he had been scrambling about trying to put an end to it, he still didn't have any idea who the partner was.

"That's the problem...," Kuroe replied. "We don't have so much as a shred of information on Ao's marriage partner."

"That's pretty strange, isn't it? You would have thought *someone* would at least know his name."

"Indeed. Perhaps Ao is intentionally concealing it. I'll have Knight Hildegarde look into it a little more, but if she can't find anything of interest, I suspect we'll have to give up on this approach."

"Right... So what's the other suggestion?" Mushiki asked.

"Yes," Kuroe responded, folding her middle finger so that only her index finger remained outstretched. "This one is a bit simpler and more direct."

"Hmm?"

"Lady Saika will smash through any opponents that stand in her way, then it will be case closed."

"Kuroe."

Mushiki broke out into a cold sweat at this overly militant proposal, delivered in a flat, emotionless voice.

"I'm joking."

"It didn't sound like a joke."

"It would be a major headache for any mage to start actively opposing these plans, let alone someone of Lady Saika's caliber. Then again, it wouldn't be beyond the realm of possibility to leave no witnesses, or to frame it all as Clara Tokishima's doing..."

"Kuroe."

"I'm joking," she said again, sticking out her tongue.

Her eyes, however, were far from playful.

"Well, going up against Ao means making enemies of everyone here at the Ark. It won't be an easy challenge. Think of this only as a last resort."

"That's...fine," Mushiki breathed out, embarrassed by his own naivete.

Then, with perfect timing, the school bell sounded throughout the Ark.

"Oh, is it five already?" Kuroe muttered as she glanced at the clock hanging on the wall.

"That's unusual," Mushiki began. "Ruri isn't one to be late to a—"

"...L-Li'l Saika... Li'l Kuroe...?" a voice came from their earpieces. "C-can you hear me...?"

"Hilde. Did something happen?" Mushiki asked.

"W-we have a big problem...," she responded in a panic. "I was monitoring security footage from inside the Ark just now...and Ruri was being led away by a bunch of girls wearing those weird masks...!"

"...Wh-what?" Mushiki exclaimed, breaking into a tense frown. "What do you mean? Ruri's been taken away by the Azures?"

"On Ao's orders, no doubt," Kuroe said. "But for what reason?"

"U-um... One of the masked girls... Er, she said something about the wedding date being moved up..."

"...!"

Mushiki and Kuroe both caught their breath.

"Lady Saika."

"Right... Let's go." Mushiki nodded as he rose quickly from his chair.

Behind the Ark's central school building was a magnificent bamboo grove, so beautiful that one could easily forget that they were at the bottom of the ocean.

Following the path that runs directly through the middle of it, one will eventually come across a tall wall punctuated by a huge gate.

Within lay the compound of the prestigious Fuyajoh clan, the site of their main family's residence.

Though it was situated within the Ark, the area beyond the gate was considered private property, and neither students nor teachers were permitted to enter. The only individuals allowed inside, with the exception of members of the Fuyajoh family themselves, were the members of the disciplinary committee who had been assigned to it as security.

Even Kuroe seemed largely unaware of what precisely took place within its walls.

Given the special environment of the Ark and the absolute authority and power that Ao Fuyajoh wielded, the premise essentially enjoyed extensive extraterritorial privileges.

To give an extreme example, should some kind of incident take place within the Fuyajoh family—even something that resulted in the death of one of its members—the consequences would be decided by Ao alone.

A hidden garden that once you enter, you could never leave. The belly of a man-eating demon.

Among mages outside the Ark, the place had taken on a reputation almost of a ghost story. That was the kind of impression people had of it.

"...Ruri is here?" Mushiki whispered, standing atop the wall that separated the school district from the grounds of the Fuyajoh residence.

"Y-yep... Definitely. I don't know what's going on inside...but Ruri seems to be in the main building's ceremony hall...," Hildegarde reported.

Kuroe pulled out her cell phone and showed it to Mushiki. The screen showed a floor plan situated amid the vast grounds, complete with blue markings.

"Way to go, Hilde."

"...Tee-hee... I-it's all for Ruri...," she responded, her chuckle sounding awkward even through the remote earpiece.

"How's security?" Mushiki asked.

"Ah...right. There seem to be a lot of those masked girls out and about..."

"I see. They must be on guard against Lady Saika," Kuroe said. "Knight Hildegarde. Can you hack the security cameras to show nothing out of the ordinary, like you did so Ruri could come to Lady Saika's quarters?"

"I-it shouldn't be im*possible*... But this time, they're specifically on the watch for an intruder, assuming one will try to break in... It might not be very effective..."

"Hmm...this is going to be a nuisance," Kuroe mumbled as she stroked her chin.

"Er...um..." Hildegarde breathed. "So...instead of trying to get you in unnoticed, it might be better just to mess around with their systems..."

"Ah."

"L-leave it to me...Li'l Saika, Li'l Kuroe."

"Got it. We're in your hands," Mushiki replied.

Hildegarde gave them a shy smile before cutting the line.

"Now then, Lady Saika. We need to confirm one last thing."

"What's that?"

"I suggested using force earlier, but it would be no laughing matter if you invaded the premises of the Fuyajoh residence and whisked Ruri away. It would likely be regarded as an act of hostility to the Fuyajoh clan, an unjustified interference. Even for you, if this were to come to light, you would be faced with criticism from all quarters... So, despite all that, are you still going to save Ruri?" Kuroe asked matter-of-factly.

She was probably right. No matter how powerful a mage Saika might be, others would hardly tolerate such reckless, unprincipled behavior. This course of action was sure to be to Saika's disadvantage, and it was far from Mushiki's intention to sully her reputation.

"..."

Mushiki switched off his earpiece and turned to Kuroe. Then, in his own voice, he said, "Can I say something?"

Kuroe followed suit by deactivating her own earpiece, before responding as Saika, "What is it?"

"...First, I'm sorry. This is between me and Ruri. I'm sorry for getting Saika involved in it all."

"Hmm. So?"

"On top of that, please—lend me your strength," Mushiki said. "I don't know if I can make up for the damage that Saika is going to suffer because of this. But I'll do everything I can. So please, help me save my sister... Help me save Ruri."

Kuroe lowered her gaze. "I see. I understand your feelings, Mushiki Kuga. Then let me ask you one thing."

"Please," he answered, staring straight back at her.

Then, with Kuroe's usual expression and voice, Saika asked, "How would Lady Saika respond to that request?"

"..."

Following her example, Mushiki returned to the role that had been given to him.

"Kuroe."

"Yes?"

"...That's a stupid question."

Then, without the slightest hesitation, he kicked off from the wall and leaped into the air.

As her older brother, it was true—he couldn't leave Ruri to her fate. But just as importantly...

He couldn't accept that Saika would stand by and do nothing while a beloved student was sent off to be married against her will.

"Well said," Kuroe answered, following behind him.

"A-3, all clear."

"B-1, all clear."

"C-5, all clear."

The atmosphere was tense inside the security room on the grounds of the main Fuyajoh residence.

The space was filled with ten or so members of the disciplinary committee, each monitoring live video feeds on countless computer monitors. There was an unprecedented level of tension in their voices as they exchanged reports.

But that was understandable. After all, Ruri Fuyajoh's wedding ceremony was about to take place in the ceremony hall at the far end of the compound.

It was no exaggeration to say that nuptials were one of the most important ceremonies for the Fuyajoh clan. It would be an utter disaster if they should end in failure.

But that wasn't their only reason for concern.

No, the main reason behind their heightened heart rates was the presence of outsiders meaning to sabotage the event.

"…I wonder if she'll really show up…," one of the Azures murmured from behind her mask.

Judging by her tone, one might have guessed that she doubted the very existence of this fabled interloper—or perhaps this was merely a show of bravado prompted by the tense atmosphere.

"Even for that Madam Witch from the Garden, she'll be in for a huge headache if she tries to interfere with the ceremony. She could even end up losing her position as headmistress. She would be stupid to take such a massive risk for the sake of a single student."

A hushed commotion ensued at this last remark—only for another Azure to raise her voice to reprimand them. "I'll pretend I didn't hear that just now. Get back to monitoring surveillance. You should know she's not a foe to let your guard down around."

"But—"

"Have you forgotten what Lady Ao said? We're dealing with Saika Kuozaki here. There's no telling what she might—"

At that moment, the Azure watching the live video feed fell silent.

There had been, it seemed, a discrepancy in the video stream from one of the security cameras.

"Huh…?"

The Azure furrowed her brow, moving closer to the screen to make sure.

The image showed the garden around the main residence building. And there was unmistakably a silhouette that had entered the frame.

For a moment, she thought it might be Saika Kuozaki—but she was wrong. It clearly wasn't a human being. It was huge, but tall and slender, and though shaped like a four-legged creature, its neck was unusually long.

The unidentified animal ran toward the camera, its head bobbing and shaking atop its long neck. The Azure couldn't help letting out a shocked gasp at this sudden and bewildering sight.

But that wasn't all.

The walls of the security room were covered in monitors—and they all reflected similar creatures.

"What…?"

"What the hell is going on here…?"

One after the next, the monitors were all displaying a host of strange monsters.

After a moment, the Azures realized what they were facing—the creatures were the result of crudely rendered CGI.

"Huh…? The security system has been hacked…?!"

"What?! Restart the system at once!"

"Hold on! Check on the situation at the residence first! Has anyone contacted security?!"

"C-communications are down…!"

All at once, the room descended into chaos.

Yet the first Azure to have noticed something wrong on the monitors continued to stare at the certain dancing *something* on the display.

"…Why a giraffe…?" she whispered in a stunned voice.

Mushiki and Kuroe followed Hildegarde's directions, running through the grounds of the Fuyajoh residence in the evening twilight.

It had been some time since they had passed over the wall, but there was still no sign of any alarm sounding. Avoiding the path and weaving their way through the bamboo grove, they finally reached a vantage point looking out at the sprawling compound.

"Hmm. So that's it," Mushiki observed.

"It seems so. I never expected to get this far without meeting opposition. Excellent work, Knight Hildegarde."

"*Tee-hee…*" Hildegarde giggled in embarrassment at Kuroe's praise. "*B-but be careful. I'm sure there will be lots of guards around the main building—*"

But before she could finish her sentence—

"—?! Headmistress Kuozaki…?!" sounded a voice to their right.

Glancing around, Mushiki spotted several girls dressed in masks and overcoats—members of the Azures.

"Uh-oh."

"So they spotted us immediately."

Mushiki and Kuroe both spoke calmly as the Azures slowly spread out to surround them.

"…How are you doing, Headmistress Kuozaki? You're aware this is a restricted area, I hope?" one of the girls said politely.

"Really?" Mushiki responded with a soft smile. "Do forgive the intrusion. I must have gotten lost while out for a walk. But now *you're* here, with perfect timing. Would you mind showing me around? I'd like to see the ceremony hall—where Ruri is."

"…!"

With those words, Mushiki made their intentions clear.

"Second substantiation, activate!" ordered the one who looked like the squad leader.

"*Yes!*" the others responded in unison as double-layered world crests appeared above their heads.

With that cry, spears imbued with magical blades formed in their hands.

Just as he had thought during the battle against the krakens, it was a strange sight. The Azures made use of substantiation techniques incorporating *human information* into the composition formulas. According to Kuroe, it was rare to see so many people using such similar substantiations.

Well, to a certain extent, it wasn't impossible to alter the shape and design of one's natural substantiations. These young women were clearly trained for group combat. No doubt they had intentionally aligned their abilities to one another to establish coherent tactics.

"Engage!"

But while Mushiki was busy pondering their substantiations, an angry voice sounded out, and the Azures around him rushed in all at once.

"Lady Saika," Kuroe said.

"…All right," he responded, raising his right hand forward and narrowing his eyes. "Second Substantiation: Stellarium."

At that moment—

A double-layered world crest appeared over Mushiki's head, and a huge staff equipped with an earth-shaped orb at its end manifested in his hand.

Then, as he struck the ground with the end of the staff…

"Wh-what the…?!"

The countless bamboo trees around them twisted and writhed like snakes, binding the hands and feet of the Azures who had sought to attack him.

"H-huh…?!"

"G-gah!"

The Azures flailed their arms and legs in an effort to escape the restraints, but soon their entire bodies were bound tightly by the bamboos, and they lost consciousness.

"Phew…"

Surveying the aftermath, Mushiki let out a small sigh.

Saika's second substantiation, Stellarium, had the power to transform the world, albeit only to limited extents. It could be used in practically any shape and form, depending on the user's imagination.

Her fourth substantiation was immensely powerful but also consumed a great deal of magical energy, and so it carried high risk. And this time, his opponents were other people. It would be too dangerous to attempt to use it when his level of control was far from perfect. He had spent a good deal of his downtime practicing Saika's techniques with Kuroe, so that he could snatch victory where possible using only his first and second substantiations. He had been a little worried, but the situation seemed to have worked itself out.

"How was that, Kuroe?"

"Look up, Lady Saika!"

Just as Mushiki was about to turn back to Kuroe, she cried out in alarm—and so, catching his breath, he turned his hand upward.

The next moment, a sharp sound rang out as a tremendous impact made contact with his arm.

From up above, an Azure wielding a sword forged by magic was flying toward him.

"Hmm..."

With a frown, Mushiki swatted the attacker away—the masked girl was sent flying through the air before landing on her feet.

Without lowering her guard, the young woman raised her weapon and called out: "...Are you mad, Headmistress Kuozaki? I didn't think you would try to strong-arm us!"

From her voice, Mushiki recognized the girl as Asagi, his eyes narrowing as he raced to control his breathing.

"Strong-arm you? It seems there's been a misunderstanding."

"A misunderstanding...?"

"Your disciplinary committee is composed of students at the Ark, no? I thought I would give you all a special lesson in the form of a real-life battle... You won't have many chances to face Saika Kuozaki directly. So brace yourself."

"Enough with the jokes...!" Asagi choked in anger, kicking the ground running as she charged toward him.

"Stellarium!" he intoned, raising his staff to meet her.

With a flash of brilliant color, countless fresh bamboos flexed their trunks to ensnare her.

"Faster...!"

But Asagi leapt backward to avoid the flurry of roving bamboos and, with the same momentum, swung the sword forged by her second substantiation.

However, she was too far away. The bluish-white blade succeeded only in drawing a luminous arc through the air.

But then—

"...!"

Mushiki's breath caught in his throat. Asagi's blade seemed to warp and melt, extending out like a whip.

"Gah…!"

His reaction was one heartbeat too slow.

But before the tip of the sword could reach his chest—

"Tch…!"

Asagi leapt backward, the writhing blade extending from her hand likewise falling back.

It wasn't long before Mushiki understood why.

Kuroe had leapt forward with an upper roundhouse kick.

"Oh? You did well to dodge that one," she said.

"You…" Asagi grabbed the hilt of her sword, hoping to attack with her blade once more.

But it wasn't meant to be.

She was thrown off balance, and a rich explosion of magic in every color of the rainbow burst out around her forehead.

"—."

Mushiki's attack had caused cracks in Asagi's mask.

Just like that, she lost consciousness, falling flat on her back—the world crest vanishing from above her head and the sword in her right hand fading away, too.

"…Sorry, Kuroe. You saved me there."

"Not at all. This is a part of an attendant's job… Good work, Lady Saika. You're getting quite good at using your first and second substantiations, I see," she responded with a refreshing grin.

Mushiki flashed a wry smile, before turning his gaze to the fallen Asagi. "She's good, as expected of someone in charge of the Ark's security… But that second substantiation—why do I feel like I've seen it somewhere before…?"

Suddenly, he stopped.

The reason was simple enough—Asagi's broken mask fell away, exposing its wearer's face for the first time.

"—Huh…?" he exclaimed, his eyes opening wide as he let out a dumb gasp completely out of character for Saika Kuozaki.

But you couldn't blame him for acting so surprised. Anyone would have reacted the same way under those circumstances.

After all—

"…R-Ruri…?"

The face beneath the mask was none other than that of his sister, Ruri Fuyajoh.

"Huh… Hey, wh-what's going on here…?" he murmured in a stunned voice, completely forgetting to play the part of Saika in tone and demeanor.

"…"

Kuroe did not reproach him; instead she bent down next to Asagi with a frown as she reached out to touch her cheeks.

"Ruri should be in the ceremony hall. Could it be a disguise…? No, that's not likely… It can't be…"

Seemingly having realized something, she rose to her feet and approached the other Azures, still unconscious and bound by the bamboo trees.

Then, reaching out to the masks that they were wearing, one by one, she peeled them off to expose their faces.

"What…?"

The sight made Mushiki catch his breath.

The Azures had been unmasked, and they each had Ruri's face.

"Kuroe? What's going on here?"

"…I can't say for sure. But I have a bad feeling about this. We should hurry to the ceremony hall," she said, letting the masks in her hand drop to the ground as she turned to the main residence at the end of the bamboo grove.

"…Ugh…"

In between rituals in the innermost sanctum of the Fuyajoh mansion, Ruri broke out into a frown and gritted her teeth.

Or more precisely, that was the most she could presently do. Some kind of magic seemed to be inhibiting her movements. From the neck down, she couldn't move her body at will, and she sat in a formal *seiza* position.

"..."

Hoping to gather more information, Ruri's eyes darted everywhere.

It was a large room, with a mysterious pattern drawn over the wooden floor. A strange atmosphere filled the air. There were no lights, and even though she was clearly indoors, a large bonfire was burning.

Next, she turned her gaze downward—and found herself wrinkling her brow.

She couldn't help it. After all, she was wearing a splendid pure white kimono.

Yes, Ruri had been abducted by members of the Azures while enroute to Saika's guest quarters and forced to take a bath before being changed into this wedding dress.

There could only be one possible reason for all this—the wedding ceremony that was supposed to take place in several days' time must have been moved up in response to Saika's visit to the Ark.

Then—

"...!"

Her eyebrow twitched.

Ring, ring...

From somewhere in the distance, she could hear the faint sound of a small bell.

"What...is that sound...?"

She pulled a quizzical face, the sound growing louder and louder until it entered the room in front of her.

Slowly, the door began to slide open.

A woman in a beautiful white robe stepped inside, holding a folded fan in one hand with her face hidden behind a veil. On either side of her, two masked girls dressed in shrine maiden outfits and holding sets of kagura bells followed reverently.

Ruri's eyes burned with resentment at this sight.

"...Lady Ao."

"Yes... That dress suits you, Ruri. You're beautiful," said the woman in the kimono—Ao Fuyajoh—as though deeply moved.

Ruri couldn't make out her expressions due to the veil and the darkness of the room, but she could sense the woman was smiling.

"…Let me ask you this. What on earth are you planning to do with me?"

"Let me answer you… We're about to hold the nuptial ceremony," Ao responded, throwing her words back at her.

Ruri glared at her. "You're stubborn… I will never, *ever* give you what you want. This *nuptial ceremony* or whatever you want to call it—go ahead, but I'm not going to just accept some lifelong partner because of some moldy old ritual. I'll beat the crap out of any husband you pick out for me and leave."

Ao sighed, as if trying to cover up her anxiety. "That won't do. Having spirit is all well and good, but you need to know when to show grace… Because you're going to be the head of the Fuyajoh clan from now on."

"…Huh?"

Ruri frowned, with absolutely no idea what on earth she was saying.

At that, Ao smiled, and began to slowly remove her veil.

"What…?"

Ruri couldn't help gasping when she saw Ao's face.

"Now…let the nuptial ceremony begin."

Ao's mouth twisted into a smile—and the sound of the kagura bells in the hands of the masked girls filled the room.

"Hilde—how much farther to the ceremony hall?"

"Y-you're nearly there… It's the room at the end of that corridor…!" Hildegarde's voice sounded from their earpieces as they ran down the long corridor in the main Fuyajoh residence.

Following her directions, Mushiki poured yet more strength into his legs as he charged forward.

"Let's hurry."

"Right," Kuroe answered behind him.

After defeating Asagi and the other Azures in the bamboo grove, Mushiki and Kuroe had run into security guards twice in the main residence. Using Saika's powers, they had successfully neutralized all opponents, but there could be no mistaking that it was taking them longer to reach Ruri than they had anticipated.

Having seen the faces of the Azures, Asagi included, Mushiki couldn't shake an indescribable sense of unease. He pushed forward, hoping to reach Ruri as quickly as possible.

Then—

"Hah!"

Having reached their destination, Mushiki kicked the door in without hesitation.

From the moment they had entered the Fuyajoh residence, he hadn't expected things to go smoothly.

If Ao, the head of the Fuyajoh clan, and the other members of the family, too, were all on the other side of the door, then he was determined to face them to rescue Ruri.

...But what he found on the other side was beyond his wildest expectations.

In the center of the large room, decorated all over with arcane patterns, sat Ruri alone with her back to them, dressed in a white kimono.

Mushiki glanced around, but there were no other figures in sight. Ruri's shadow flickered strangely from the light of a bonfire by the far wall.

"Ruri!" he called out, rushing to her side. "Ruri, are you okay?"

"Madam...Witch..."

Though he shook her shoulders, Ruri stared back at him in a daze.

"What...am I doing here...?" she asked, her memory cloudy.

Perhaps she was under the influence of some kind of magic, Mushiki wondered.

He was concerned about her condition, but their first priority was to get out of here. He took her hand, pulling her to her feet.

"Can you walk? We can't afford to waste our time here. We need to leave the Ark now," he said, tugging at her hand and turning toward the way they had come.

Yet—

"Lady Saika!" Kuroe yelled from behind him.

"...?!"

Mushiki glanced around—and at that moment, a magical blade grazed past his side. Choking on his breath, he leapt backward to safety.

"...Oh, a pity. Good job...dodging that just now..."

"...R-Ruri...?" Mushiki stammered in a faint voice as he pressed a hand to the sharp pain at his side.

Behind him stood Ruri, her two-stage world crest hovering above her head, armed with a naginata—its blade burning like demon fire.

He could hardly believe his eyes at first, but Ruri had evidently activated her second substantiation and attacked him.

"My Luminous Blade... The shape is a little different, but it's similar enough. Interesting." Ruri spoke with deep emotion, turning her summoned second substantiation around in her hand like a toy.

The blue blade flickered through the air as she spun it from side to side.

"Are you all right, Lady Saika?" Kuroe asked.

"...Ah," Mushiki answered, glancing down at the hand at his side.

The wound was light, but the blade nonetheless seemed to have pierced his skin. His palm was stained with blood.

"..."

Though filled with burning rage at the thought of Saika's body sustaining injury, Mushiki managed to suppress his emotions. If he acted out of anger here, he might inadvertently cause her even more harm.

"What—*who*—are you?" Mushiki asked the girl with Ruri's face, his gaze sharpening.

Looking closely, he couldn't consider the person in front of him anyone other than Ruri. Unlike the Azures, she didn't just have a face *like* Ruri's—this was unmistakably Ruri herself.

But that should have been impossible.

After all, the real Ruri would never turn her weapon against Saika.

"Heh..." The girl sneered. "Don't be absurd, Madam Witch. Have you forgotten the face of your beloved student?" she joked.

Annoyed, Mushiki frowned. "Don't play games with me. You're not Ruri."

"Heh-heh... I'm not playing anything. I'm Ruri Fuyajoh. Really... *In the flesh*, at least."

"What...?" Mushiki breathed suspiciously.

Then, from behind, Kuroe's voice caught in her throat. "...No. The *nuptial ceremony...*"

"Oh? Your attendant is very perceptive, it seems." The girl smiled as she rested a hand on her chest. "The Fuyajoh clan's nuptial ceremony isn't about marrying into some man's family—it's a ritual to select a new Ao Fuyajoh from amid the clan's current members."

"What...?" Mushiki's eyes widened in alarm.

Selecting a new Ao Fuyajoh—somehow, Mushiki knew that she didn't mean picking someone to succeed as head of the family.

At that moment, he realized it—the speech patterns and mannerisms of the Ruri in front of him were virtually identical to those of Ao Fuyajoh.

Then, putting his worst suspicions into words, Kuroe muttered: "...A transferring technique—moving one's soul into another body... There's an ancient story of a mage who tried to live forever by transferring their soul from their own aged body into a younger one to remain in their prime..."

"'Aged body'? What a dreadful turn of phrase." The girl—Ao—chuckled.

It was an eerie expression, certainly not one that Ruri would ever make. It rubbed him the wrong way and left him feeling uncomfortable.

"...So basically, Ao has usurped Ruri's body?"

"To put it simply, yes," Kuroe said grimly. "...But just like organ transplantation, there's always a risk of incompatibility between soul and body. In that story I mentioned earlier, the mage's new body couldn't endure the transfer and ultimately destroyed itself, killing the mage. It's no easy feat, changing bodies on a regular basis..."

Kuroe paused, furrowing her brow in sudden realization. "...The Azures...," she muttered.

"...Oh?" Ao's eyebrow twitched in response. "So you worked that out, too? You're quite the clever little thing, aren't you now?"

"...What do you mean?" Mushiki asked in a low voice.

"...You saw them," Kuroe responded, watching Ao closely. "The Azures all had the same face. Like they're all copies of the same person."

"Ah..." Mushiki nodded in recollection.

So many different girls all with Ruri's face lying unconscious on the ground had certainly been a nightmarish sight.

"Earlier, I said soul and body need to be compatible. In other words, if you prepare countless bodies that you *know* to be compatible with your soul, you can swap for a younger one whenever you want... And the body most compatible with your soul will always be your own."

"...No way..." Mushiki narrowed his eyes at Kuroe's explanation.

Then, Ao spread her hands as she met his gaze head on. "Indeed. The Azures are all clones of Ao Fuyajoh. They are all members of the Fuyajoh clan, the spears who protect the sea and govern the Ark."

"—."

This shocking revelation left Mushiki momentarily speechless.

But it wasn't long before a question rose to his lips. "Nonsense. What about Ruri then?"

"Ruri, strictly speaking, isn't *fully me*. Some of my clones end up bearing children with men from outside. Creating new branch families, so to speak. But the children born that way tend to inherit more of my characteristics. Though as the generations go by, those elements seem to be gradually fading away," Ao said, resting a hand on her chest.

She was practically claiming that Ruri's body was hers to do with as she pleased.

Mushiki glared at her, gritting his teeth.

"...So you transferred your soul to the body of your strongest descendent. That's all this is, isn't it?"

"You don't need to glare at me. For a woman of the Fuyajoh clan, becoming my vessel is the fulfillment of her life's purpose. There could be no greater joy, you understand? After all, they were each born to replace me. In fact, she ought to be grateful that I would deign to clothe myself in the flesh of a runaway," Ao said with a repulsive grin.

Mushiki could hardly contain his antipathy. "...Kuroe?" he murmured.

She understood his implied meaning at once. "...It hasn't been long since the transfer was conducted, so Ruri's consciousness shouldn't have disappeared yet. If Ao's soul could be stripped away from the body, it might be possible to free her."

"...I see." He nodded, turning back to Ao. "Your ritual seems to be over. Which I suppose means you're free now... But I don't exactly have all the time in the world here. I came all the way to the bottom of the sea to visit this place. It wouldn't hurt for me to offer you a gift at the very least," he said, raising his right hand in front of him.

Then, with perfect timing, a two-layered world crest appeared above his head, his staff rematerializing in his hand.

Seeing that, Ao crouched down, readying her naginata.

Electrifying tension filled the air between the two of them.

"...This does come as something of a surprise," Ao muttered.

"...What does?"

"I thought you, of all people, would understand, Saika."

At that moment—

Ao's naginata blade swelled like a blazing flame, transforming into countless needles all shooting Mushiki's way.

"Hmm..."

With a frown, he slammed the base of his staff against the floor—and in a split second, the wood in the room began to undulate and ripple, morphing into a barrier directly in front of him. The myriad of brilliant needles crashed into it, stopped in their tracks.

"Heh..."

But it didn't end there. Ao stepped forward and twisted her body, swinging her Luminous Blade in a wide arc and sending its long, thin, formless knife-edge dancing through the air.

Within moments, the blade was near Mushiki's neck, forcing him to turn his body to dodge it in the nick of time.

"Stellarium...!" he wheezed, holding his staff out at an unnatural angle.

All types of objects within his field of vision began to warp and shift as though imbued with minds of their own, reaching out toward his opponent.

"Tepid," Ao sneered, brushing aside his counterattacks with a wide sweep of her weapon.

Her blade was as flexible as water, with an unparalleled sharpness, and as hot as fire—an impossible combination.

Having watched Ruri fight beside him, Mushiki had thought that he understood her abilities—but confronted by this foe now, he realized that he had been naive in his thinking.

Pure and intangible. An infinitely changing ability that could respond to any situation. The strongest manifestation of Ruri Fuyajoh's genius.

Even though she had only just usurped her body, Ao's skill in handling it was no less extraordinary.

"..."

Mushiki's shoulders heaved with his labored breathing.

Ao, guarding herself with her naginata, narrowed her eyes in suspicion. "Are you really Saika?" she asked, repeating the question she had thrown his way after the school principals' meeting.

Mushiki was startled for a moment but quickly responded with a wry smile. "...I wonder. Perhaps there's someone else inside me, just like with you?" he said in jest.

Ao snorted with laughter. "You seem too weak to be the Saika I know. Your techniques are certainly powerful, but that's it. I don't feel threatened in the slightest. Does that speak to the hidden potential of Ruri's body? Or...perhaps the vaunted Witch of Resplendent Color won't go all out against the body of a beloved student?" she spat back, squinting in distaste. "I would have been happy if you had given up and run home... But I can't stand being made light of like this. Perhaps I'll give this new body a little test drive and keep you company for a short while."

Then, making a sign with her hand, she intoned, "Third Substantiation: Rays of the Rising Sun."

A three-layered world crest reminiscent of an ogre's horns unfurled above Ao's head—and at the same time, her body erupted in blue flames, covering her in fiery armor.

Her third substantiation, assimilation-rank—a battle form in which a mage wrapped themselves in the product of their substantiations.

"Lady Saika!" Kuroe shouted.

"...Right!"

One's odds in battle were never good against a mage who had manifested their third substantiation.

Mushiki organized his thoughts as he responded, "Third Substantiation: Animaclad...!"

Likewise, Mushiki's third world crest appeared over his head; his body glowed with a radiance of brilliant color as a majestic dress unfurled around him.

Watching on, Ao broke into a satisfied grin. "I'm glad you're responding in the same manner. Your third substantiation is as charming as ever. I can't help but admire it."

"...Yours looks splendid, too. I did want to see Ruri pull it off herself, though."

After that short flippant exchange, they both launched themselves toward each other and resumed their battle.

The armor-clad Ao was no longer the person she had been a moment ago. This was why the third level of substantiation technique was known as *assimilation*—a mage essentially transformed, their body possessing physical abilities above and beyond those of regular human beings.

With her leg strength and kinetic vision sharpened to their utmost, Ao unleashed an onslaught of attacks faster than the eye could see. For regular onlookers, it would have been virtually impossible to catch her movements.

"Hah...!"

But Mushiki had also activated his third substantiation, and while still inexperienced, he was the world's strongest mage, Saika Kuozaki. Somehow, armed with the staff of his second substantiation, he managed to respond to each of his foe's attacks.

And so the two mages, each a headmistress of her own school, faced off against each other with their third substantiations, a vortex of magical energy raging through the ceremony hall like a whirlwind.

"Hmm…"

In the middle of this extreme situation, Mushiki somehow found time to ponder.

His opponent was Ao Fuyajoh, champion of the ocean. Her strength and ability were plain to see. Right now, it took everything he had simply to use Saika's techniques to block her attacks.

The only way he could get Ruri back would be to make Ao admit defeat and use her transfer technique once again.

…But would that really be possible?

If he was to have any hope of pulling it off, his fourth substantiation would be the only way. But if he miscalculated and lost control, he could cause Ruri's body irreparable damage. What then? Or worse, what if he ended up taking her life…?

"…—."

Mushiki caught his breath as his imagination got the better of him.

It was at that moment that he heard Kuroe calling out behind him, "Lady Saika! The amount of magical power you're emitting is increasing! You need to calm yourself!"

"…!"

Mushiki was startled. Right, the amount of magical energy that emitted from his body varied depending on his state of mind. If he ended up reverting to his original body now, he wouldn't have even the slightest chance of winning this fight.

But that momentary hesitation had left him open—dangerously so.

"Well, this *is* a one-sided affair."

A second after Ao's voice rang out, she appeared before him, bearing down her Luminous Blade.

Stretching out from its hilt was a blade longer than he had ever seen before, extending in a straight line until it almost pierced the wall of the ceremony room. He could think of it only as a giant's sword.

"Luminous Blade: Brand."

With those words, a flash of light cut through the walls and ceiling of the hall, filling Mushiki's vision with blue flames.

He didn't quite remember what had happened.

He didn't even know what he had done.

When Mushiki came to his senses, a young Ruri was crying before him.

...! Mushiki! Mushiki!

Her perfectly round eyes were filled with tears, and she clung to his chest.

Mushiki gently stroked her hair, flashing her a warm smile.

Don't worry. I'll protect you, Ruri.

"...Ah..."

Mushiki awoke to a light tap on his cheek—his eyes shooting open as he took in the situation.

The first thing he noticed was that his body had returned to its original state.

Next, he realized that he was lying amid shadows—and that in front of him, Kuroe had swung her hand down to slap him.

"You're awake," she said.

"...Thank you." Mushiki stood up as he rubbed his cheeks.

Staring back at her, he noticed that her clothes were scorched here and there. She must have rescued him from Ao's attack at the last minute.

"...Sorry. Thanks for saving me."

"Not at all. But be careful. This isn't over yet," she said, glancing up to look at the crumbling walls.

Mushiki followed her line of sight—to take in the Fuyajoh main residence, half destroyed by Ao's last attack. A huge amount of rubble and debris filled the area, while blue flames continued to burn in a few places. Depending on how you looked at it, you might even describe it as a mystical spectacle.

In the center of all that rubble stood Ao Fuyajoh, still clad in her armor and holding her naginata in her hands.

She probably suspected Saika had escaped her last attack and was lurking somewhere nearby waiting for a chance to counter. So she remained on guard, scrutinizing the area.

Naturally, her profile was still that of Ruri herself. Mushiki winced in pain, his heart aching.

"…We need to save Ruri quickly. Kuroe, please. I need more—"

But before he could finish, Kuroe pressed a finger against his lips to silence him.

"No," she answered.

"Kuroe…?" His eyes widened in alarm. "Wh-why not? In my own body, I won't stand a chance…"

"Hmm. So you're saying you could win if you transform into Lady Saika?"

"W-well…"

Mushiki swallowed his words, hearing her put it so bluntly. After all, he had lost just now even using Saika's third substantiation.

"But that doesn't mean I can just give up, right? It's unforgivable, usurping someone's body like that."

"…Does that make *me* unforgivable as well?"

"Huh…?"

Mushiki frowned, caught off guard by Kuroe's response in Saika's voice.

"Ao makes copies of herself and changes bodies on a regular basis… Yes, from an ethical perspective, there are many problems with that. But then, shouldn't you denounce me, too, for using a synthetic body?" she said with self-directed scorn as she rested a hand on her chest.

"—."

Only then did Mushiki realize the reason behind the déjà vu he had felt when hearing about Ao's soul-transferring technique.

Right. Saika had transferred her own soul into an artificial body, a homunculus, to prolong her life.

"B-but...Kuroe's body...didn't have a soul...right?"

"...Indeed... But if it did, what then? Would it be better if I had left this world?"

"...—."

Mushiki's voice caught in his throat. Nonetheless, it didn't take long for him to come up with a response: "So you're saying if I accept your continued existence, I've got to accept Ao's methods and give up on Ruri?"

"..."

Saika remained silent for a moment before answering, "If I *did* say that, what would you do?"

"..."

Mushiki took a deep breath, then shook his head.

"That premise doesn't add up."

"...Oh? Do explain."

"Saika would never say such a thing."

At this, Saika shrugged in exasperation. "There's no point trying to tease you, is there?"

"I'm sorry. But I could tell from the face you were making that you didn't mean any of that."

"...And what sort of face was that?" Saika responded, touching her cheeks.

In spite of the situation, Mushiki couldn't help breaking out into a smile.

She must have sensed as much herself, as she let out a soft cough to regain her composure, then continued in Kuroe's reserved voice, "In the end, this struggle is the result of individual selfishness. Each of us here have their own reasons and individual circumstances. Good and evil belong only to the realm of fairy tales and the like... Our foe is Ao Fuyajoh, the head of the Fuyajoh clan. She's no ordinary opponent. If you want to win against her, you must be prepared to lay waste to her feelings and everything she holds dear... Mushiki,

I ask you again: Do you still want to save Ruri? No matter the consequences?"

"...Yes," he answered, looking her squarely in the eyes.

It was far from his intention to give her a light, carefree response. He was simply saying that he had already decided to come to Ruri's aid, no matter what.

Kuroe must have sensed as much from his expression, as she lowered her gaze. "Very well," she responded with a nod. "Then let's return to the arena."

"Right. I'll need you to help me undergo another state change," he said, taking her by the shoulders.

Kuroe, however, pushed back strongly. "Please, let me finish. During your fight just now, I realized something while I watched Ao with my Eye of Inquiry."

"Realized what?"

"You see...," Kuroe began, lowering her voice.

"—."

In a field of burning blue rubble, Ao Fuyajoh sighed as she vigilantly watched her surroundings.

She had struck at Saika's momentary opening, hoping to deal a killing blow—but there had been no clear sign that the strike had even made contact.

No doubt her opponent had managed to avoid sustaining a direct hit somehow. After all, this was Saika Kuozaki whom she was facing. It wouldn't have been at all surprising if she had one or two tricks up her sleeve—or even a thousand or two.

Nor could she imagine that vindictive Saika merely turning tail after taking such a heavy blow. She must be hiding somewhere, biding her time. Ao poured her strength into her hand gripping her naginata as she called out, her voice echoing, "Saika? Just how long are you going to hide? You're aware that if you take too long, this body will become perfectly attuned to my soul, yes?"

She hoped to provoke her foe, to probe her weakness.

In fact, it was true that this body wasn't yet fully attuned to her soul. The longer Saika lurked in the shadows, the more it would work in Ao's favor. But even with that in mind, it would be riskier still, she determined, to give Saika the time to formulate a new plan.

Then, as if in response to her provocation, something flew out from Ao's blind spot.

"Hmph…"

Without the slightest delay, she swept her Luminous Blade to one side and cleaved through the flying object.

At that moment, there was an explosion. Her foe was probably using a technique of some sort to throw explosive projectiles.

But surely Saika would have known that such a paltry attack couldn't hope to best *her*, clad in her third substantiation. Naturally, it must have been a diversion to conceal her true actions.

Then, as if to prove her right, a figure came bolting toward her as the explosion continued to fan out.

"Saika, you fool."

But as Ao swung her Luminous Blade, she frowned.

The reason was simple—it wasn't Saika who'd emerged from the fires of the explosion.

No, it was a boy with light-colored hair and a somewhat androgynous appearance—Ruri's older brother, Mushiki Kuga, who had inexplicably disappeared earlier.

"Now, Saika!" he shouted, and at that moment—

"What?!"

A faint sound echoed from behind.

Ao panicked and spun around.

But what she found was simply Kuroe Karasuma, Saika's attendant.

"…!"

A double—no, a triple decoy. So where was Saika setting her trap…?

She asked herself—a thought born from her deep knowledge of Saika's abilities. Yet that moment of hesitation left the smallest of openings.

Mushiki, whom she had overlooked as nothing more than a distraction, took advantage of that opportunity.

"—!"

He stepped forward, closing in. She couldn't begin to fathom his intentions. Was this another diversion to give Saika an opportunity to attack? But even if so, she couldn't afford to allow an opponent, no matter their caliber, to get too close. And so, to remove the obstacle, she swept the Luminous Blade to one side.

The tip of the weapon sliced effortlessly through his body.

"...Gah...!"

He may have been a member of the Fuyajoh bloodline, but even so... Ao didn't mean to take his life, but the strike should have been more than enough to stop him in his tracks. A thin red line had appeared on his clothes, blood seeping out.

Yet—Mushiki continued to approach, without the slightest hint of hesitation.

"...R-Ruri...!"

"What...?"

She raised a quizzical eyebrow at that ghastly sight, tightening her grip on the hilt of her naginata.

She didn't want to kill him. Yet she wasn't so good-natured that she would overlook a threat coming her way. And so aiming this time for his neck, she swung her weapon once again.

Yet—

"It's okay...Ruri...I'll protect you..."

"—."

Upon hearing that, Ao's breath caught in her throat—and the Luminous Blade refused to move according to her will.

If she paused to think, it would have been natural to put her hesitation down to mere coincidence—a momentary delay caused by a discrepancy between body and soul, or that she had been caught off guard by all the distractions.

But no. It was more like the Luminous Blade itself—or rather, Ruri's body—refused to attack him.

But that didn't mean that she was in danger here. After all, she had deployed her third substantiation. No matter what kind of attack Mushiki might try, it couldn't possibly—

"...Huh?"

The next moment, Ao let out a shrill gasp at Mushiki's choice of action.

But that was only natural.

After all, instead of launching an attack, Mushiki placed a hand on Ao's cheek and pressed his lips up against her own.

Confusion engulfed her mind in response to his soft touch—and caught in this unfathomable situation, she felt her consciousness slipping.

...

In a large room, several masked young women were lined up in a row—and at the far end, behind a bamboo blind, was the figure of a woman.

Ruri, having been brought here by her mother, stood in the corner, hunched forward with her shoulders close together.

...I read your report, a voice came from behind the bamboo blind.

It belonged to Ao Fuyajoh, the head of the Fuyajoh family. The young Ruri didn't quite understand what was going on, but she could tell that Ao was an incredibly important figure.

Even to protect his sister, to think that he manifested a substantiation at the age of ten and crushed an annihilation factor... I was surprised enough to hear that Ai had given birth to a boy...but perhaps there is something here...

...

Ruri's mother kept her eyes lowered, saying nothing. But Ruri didn't find her attitude all that strange. To be honest, she hated even coming here.

All of a sudden, the masked girls sitting around them began to whisper to themselves.

Amazing. If he trains and keeps it up, just think what an incredible mage he'll be.

But he's a boy. He'll be useless as Lady Ao's vessel.

Maybe so, but becoming a great mage—isn't that enough?

And so on and so forth, the next voice adding to the last.

It sounded like they were talking about her brother. Ruri felt a little uncomfortable for some reason, though she was sure everyone was praising him.

With that, Ao cleared her throat—and the other girls fell silent.

He does indeed display formidable talent. But at the same time, he's a danger... If he continues to improve and raises his substantiation level, he may ultimately undermine his own existence.

But Lady Ao, it would be a shame to let such talent go unused.

And our mission remains to protect the world.

If he can defend the lives of others...

Once more, the masked girls spoke among themselves—and Ao let out a small, thoughtful sigh.

...!

Ruri didn't know precisely what was happening here.

But she understood—vaguely—that if she didn't act now, misfortune would befall her brother.

And so she rose to her feet, calling out in a thin, weak voice: *I—I— ...Ruri...*

Her mother rested a hand on her shoulder to stop her, but Ruri continued nonetheless: *I'll fight in my brother's place...!*

...Do you mean that? Ao asked, her head tilted in piqued interest.

Yes, she answered calmly, looking straight into the shadow on the other side of the bamboo blind. *I'll be a mage. One strong enough to beat anyone. To destroy any annihilation factor... If there are enemies in this world, I'll defeat them... And I'll become as strong as I have to. So please...* She clenched her fists. *Just let my brother live a normal life.*

...

Ao fell silent for a moment, then let out a long breath. *Let's see just how well this failed candidate can perform... Very well. I'll grant your request,* Ao said, pointing to her with her folding fan.

Filled with raw determination, Ruri clenched her fists.

Why had she remembered the events of that day after all this time?

But whatever the reason, it was clear that the memory was the key to pulling her consciousness back from the deepest depths of darkness.

"Hmm... Ugh..."

As if waking from a long sleep, her senses began to come back.

A faint sound echoing in her eardrums. A dull smell tickling her nostrils. A soft touch on her lips.

...A soft touch on her lips?

"—!"

The moment her sense of touch reestablished its connection to her consciousness, Ruri's eyes snapped open.

Only then did she realize the situation that she was in, throwing her mind into yet greater turmoil.

But that was only natural. After all, Mushiki was kissing her on the lips, passionately, like the prince in "Sleeping Beauty."

"...?! ...?!"

It made no sense. Her eyes spun. Did this mean that Mushiki hadn't been able to stop himself, that he had leaned down to kiss her sleeping figure? But when you put it like that... No, no, no, they were brother and sister! But maybe Mushiki was conflicted, too, in his own way? She didn't want to destroy their relationship. But the flame of passion burning in her heart knew no bounds—eventually, it would cross the line. So what should she do? Should she accept the kiss and embrace him back? Pretend to still be unconscious? *Tell me, Mother. Tell me, Hizumi. Tell me, the heroines of all those shoujo manga under my bed—*

Just as Ruri's mind went around in circles, the scene before her suddenly changed.

The figure kissing her seemed to glow faintly, before transforming into that of Saika.

"…?!?!?!"

Now she was even more confused—her mind so disoriented, it was like someone had cut a flap in her skull, removed her brain, scrambled it up in a blender, and poured it back in. Because that was what had just happened. Mushiki had transformed into Saika. And while kissing her to boot. It a delusion tailor-made just for her. No, it wasn't like she loved Saika in that way—she adored her as someone worthy of her respect and reverence. She had never wanted to kiss her, though. Then again, her beloved Madam Witch's lips were so delightfully soft and plump…

And so, while her brain felt like it was melting and spilling out from her ears, Ruri came to a conclusion—this was all a dream.

Yes, she was dreaming. In which case, it couldn't be helped. With that thought, a wave of relief flooded through her body.

"Ruri!"

Mushiki, having transformed back into Saika, gently caught Ruri's body before she could fall flat on the floor.

Moments later, her mouth opened slowly.

"M-Madam…Witch…?" she whispered.

"Ah. Are you all right, Ruri?" he asked with a bright smile.

With perfect timing, Kuroe ran up to the two of them. "It seems to have worked," she said, breathing a soft sigh of relief.

This had been Kuroe's secret plan.

Ao's soul hadn't yet fully settled in Ruri's body, so, she had reasoned, there was a chance that the connection between the two could be broken simply by draining her magical energy.

And Mushiki had developed the ability to absorb energy from another individual, if only to a certain extent.

Yes. Through a kiss.

While he normally used the technique only with Kuroe, with the right preparation ahead of time, it could be used to absorb magical energy from any human target.

Ultimately, it was no more than a by-product of his fusion with Saika's body—but it seemed to have done the trick here.

"Um...can I ask something weird...?" Ruri inquired, her eyes still spinning.

"Ah. Go on," he said, breathing a sigh of relief.

"...Madam Witch. Weren't you Mushiki just now?"

"..."

Mushiki averted his gaze, as did Kuroe.

...Right. This had been the only way to take Ruri's body back from Ao, but it did present a major problem—he had now transformed right in front of her eyes.

"Huh? Why are you looking away...? H-hold on... Um...y-you... kissed me, right? And then Mushiki *changed*...into you..."

"Ruri," he said with a gentle smile as he pecked her on the forehead. "It sounds like you had an interesting dream. Sleepyhead."

"A dream...? Ah...right...I must have been dreaming..." Ruri closed her eyes in relief, then: "Hold on! A-as if! Nggghhh!"

Nope. She leaped to her feet like an unfurling spring, her cheeks blushing as her eyes shot open.

"What...? Wh-wh-wh-wh-wh-what's going on here?! So Madam Witch is Mushiki?! Or Mushiki is Madam Witch?! Ngh?! Ugh?!" She paused, quivering in sudden remembrance. "C-come to think of it, didn't Mushiki kiss Clara in the fight below the library?! I thought I must have been imagining things, but I saw Mushiki change into you there, too!"

"..."

He glanced at Kuroe in consternation.

Kuroe fell to pondering for a while, but eventually shook her head in apparent resignation. "Everything comes with risks. If this was the price to rescue Ruri, it can't be helped."

"...Right," Mushiki agreed with a hesitant sigh, slowly straightening his back. "Ruri. Please calm down for a moment."

As confused as she might be, there was no way she could refuse a direct request from Saika.

"...A-all right..."

Just as he had expected, she meekly became quiet.

"Thank you. I'll explain everything, I promise. But first—"

At that very moment, as if timed to interrupt him mid-sentence, the remaining portions of the Fuyajoh residence suddenly exploded.

"...! What?!"

Ruri furrowed her brow and dropped down to her haunches. Kuroe, meanwhile, turned her gaze toward the explosion without once letting down her guard.

Then, out of nowhere, a giant bird with blue flames as wings appeared, followed by a mage.

She was dressed in a fine Japanese kimono, with a two-part world crest hovering above her head.

Her face, showing indignation and wrath, was all but identical to Ruri's.

"...You did it, Saika. I don't know how, but you tore my soul from Ruri's body," she spat with resentment.

Those words—there could be no mistaking it. This was Ao Fuyajoh, head of the Fuyajoh clan, back in her original body. She must have returned to it after being separated from Ruri's.

No—probably not her *original* body, per se. Perhaps this, too, was one vessel chosen from among countless others.

"...Ao."

She, it seemed, hadn't puzzled out the relationship between Mushiki and Saika.

"Oh, won't you call it quits?" Mushiki said with the most Saika-like gesture that he could muster. "Ruri isn't yours anymore... I won't let you have her."

"...No. I *need* her. A strong body that won't succumb to any annihilation factor...!" Ao groaned, her eyes bloodshot.

Then, covering her mouth with one hand, she burst into a violent fit of coughing.

"Gah... Geh..."

"...!"

Mushiki's brow furrowed.

A great deal of blood had spilled from Ao's mouth.

"Ao. What in the world—"

But at that moment, just as Mushiki spoke—

"...?!"

The Fuyajoh residence—no, the entire Ark—was hit by a violent tremor.

Chapter 5
An Ancient Enemy, Reawakening

"What's goin' on?!"

Anviet Svarner, Knight of the Garden and a member of its teaching staff, his braided hair a downright mess, slammed open the doors to the Garden's operations center.

He was a young man in his mid-twenties. His normally harsh eyes appeared sharper than usual.

But that was understandable. After all, an alarm inidicating the highest level of warning had started sounding throughout the Garden several minutes earlier.

Void's Garden wasn't just a mage-training institute—it was also a base of operations for combating annihilation factors. When such threats emerged, the central administrative building served as headquarters for combat operations.

Indeed, several other members of staff were already busily engaged with their work.

Among them, Anviet spotted Knights Hildegarde and Erulka, and he marched right over to them.

"We're on the highest alert…? What the hell's goin' on?! Explain!"

"Eeep…!" Hildegarde trembled, her shoulders buckling as she retreated to hide behind Erulka.

"Stop being so intimidating. You'll frighten Hilde, shouting like that," Erulka said while stroking Hildegarde's hair.

Erulka—head of the Garden's medical department—wore a white doctor's coat. Though the oldest among the knights, she looked more like a junior high school student—and the discrepancy between her speech and her actions was something to behold.

"...I ain't being intimidating." Anviet frowned, letting out an annoyed sigh. "Whatever, just tell me what's goin' on."

"You see, Hilde?" Erulka said, taking charge of the conversation.

Behind her shoulder, Hildegarde stole a timid peek Anviet's way. "...Y-you could ask a little more nicely... Eeep..."

"...I'm sorry, all right? Can you tell me what's happenin'?" Anviet asked again, his cheeks twitching with every word.

Hildegarde continued to cower—though one might have sensed a hidden confidence behind her next words: "A-a little more...princely, maybe...?"

"...I need ya, okay? Can you tell me the story, kitty?"

"A-act a bit more like you're pampering me...?"

"All right, I'm gonna hit ya now." Anviet sighed, rolling his shoulders. Even he had his limits.

"Eeek!" Hildegarde shrieked, hiding behind Erulka again.

"That's enough, Hilde. This is an emergency." Erulka sighed.

"R-right... I'm sorry," Hildegarde murmured, reaching out to the central terminal.

The next moment, a three-dimensional spherical image was projected into the air.

"Huh? This thing..." Anviet furrowed his brow.

It looked like a model of the earth—but the next moment, a light lit up in the sea near Japan, the waves surging and spreading out to cover the entire planet.

Within moments, those raging waves had engulfed every island and landmass. All that remained were mountains more than three thousand meters high.

"Wh-what...?" Anviet could only observe with a scowl at the

nightmarish scene unfolding before his very eyes. "...Hey, what kinda sick joke is this?"

"I'm afraid it's no joke," Erulka explained. "This simulation is predicting the outcome of a phenomenon taking place right this very instant... In all likelihood, in less than one hour from now, most landmasses throughout the world will be swallowed up by the sea. There seems to be no way to prevent it. Our only option is to erect a wall around the Garden and hope that it holds. We're in the process of contacting mages outside the Garden to begin an emergency evacuation. Even if the cause is eliminated during the window for reversible annihilation, we won't be able to bring any dead mages back to life."

"Hold up! This is an annihilation factor?! You've gotta be kiddin' me?!" Anviet choked up, at a loss for words.

There was no way to regard a calamity as grave as this as anything other than a joke. Yet Anviet knew that the term *annihilation factor* meant anything was possible.

"I'll be damned..."

Erulka nodded in agreement. "Indeed. Annihilation Factor No. 004: Leviathan... A Mythologia defeated by Saika and the Ark's Ao Fuyajoh two hundred years ago."

In the midst of those terrifying tremors shaking the earth all around them, an alarm signaling the emergence of an annihilation factor rang out.

With the Ark thrown into a state of emergency, Mushiki and the others, standing amid the rubble of the main Fuyajoh residence, looked on in dismay as Ao coughed up blood.

"Argh... Gah..."

"...?! What...?"

Ao, and for some reason, Ruri, too, both crouched down, raising their hands to their chests. Kuroe ran to Ao, while Mushiki crouched by Ruri's side.

"Are you okay, Ruri?!"

"Yes... I don't know why, but it hurts around here all of a sudden," she said, exposing her neck.

Looking closely, Mushiki noticed there was now some kind of marking around her collarbone, a strange pattern lacerated across it, blood oozing from the cuts.

"Wh-what the...?"

Ruri had no recollection of the injury, reaching out to touch it gently with her fingertips.

Ao, it seemed, had a similar wound.

"...Headmistress Fuyajoh...is this...?" Kuroe asked, her gaze sharpening in suspicion.

"Did you notice it, too?" Mushiki asked her, doing his best to sound experienced. After all, while he might not have had any idea what the markings meant, he couldn't let Saika Kuozaki come off as ignorant while others were watching.

"Yes." Kuroe nodded, having clearly surmised the point of his question. "It's probably a poison, the result of a curse of some kind. A particularly strong one at that... Magic curse poisons work by engraving their effect into their target's very existence... There's no antidote or drug that can detoxify it. But when...? And by whom...?"

"..."

At this explanation, Ao averted her gaze, doing her best to hide the branding.

The next moment, Hildegarde's voice rang out through their earpieces: *"L-Li'l Saika! Li'l Kuroe...!"*

"...Hilde. What's going on?" Mushiki responded, pressing a hand up against his ear.

As worried as he was for Ruri and Ao, he couldn't ignore the quake that had just struck the Ark.

"S-something..." Hildegarde stammered quickly. *"From the sea... The Leviathan...has been revived."*

"The Leviathan...? Revived?" he repeated.

"...!" Ao's eyes shot open. "What...did you just...?" She staggered to her feet, wiping the blood from her mouth. Then, a moment later—

"Lady Ao!" someone screamed behind them.

Asagi rushed past Mushiki and the others like a raging gale to reach Ao.

Probably because Mushiki had shattered her mask earlier, her face, a mirror image of Ruri's, was fully exposed. She hurried to shield Ao, her expression full of alarm and anger.

"Whoa, *you* look just like me, too…?!" Ruri exclaimed, her eyes widening in astonishment.

But Asagi paid her no notice, lending Ao her shoulder to help her to her feet.

"Are you all right, Lady Ao?! Ugh… What on earth…?" She stopped, directing her deathly gaze straight at Mushiki.

Well, considering that Asagi had just found Ao on her knees coughing up blood, with Mushiki and the others standing across from her, her reaction was understandable.

"Asagi. Don't get the wrong idea. We had nothing to do with—"

But before he could clear up the misunderstanding, more masked girls gathered around her.

"Everyone, over there!"

"We'll save you, Lady Ao!"

"Huh?! Headmistress Kuozaki's people ganged up on Lady Ao?!"

All at once, countless Azures readied themselves for battle, Mushiki's protestations falling on deaf ears. It was like everyone had already decided that they were the bad guys here.

Yet—

"…Quiet!" Ao declared, the Azures falling quickly silent as though doused with icy water. "…This isn't the time. If that annihilation factor really has been revived…," she said odiously, squeezing a hand over her chest.

Only then did Mushiki notice it. Asagi and the other Azures were bleeding, too, just like Ao and Ruri.

Kuroe must have seen it, too, her eyes narrowing as she whispered something into Mushiki's ear.

And so Mushiki asked Ao, "That curse… Did you get it two hundred years ago, by any chance?"

"…"

Mushiki's question rendered Ao speechless, but she soon poured more strength into the hand gripping her kimono.

"...Your intuition is as keen as ever...," she finally said, breathing a resigned sigh.

"It's clear enough once you have all the pieces... Right, Kuroe?"

"Indeed."

Mushiki spoke as though asking for Kuroe's agreement—but in truth, he had yet to fully grasp the situation. He had simply gauged from her reaction that this was something that Saika should have known.

Kuroe stepped in to fill in the blanks: "The fact that the Azures, being duplicates of Lady Ao, and Ruri, too, all have the same poison markings proves that the curse has been engraved into Ao Fuyajoh's very essence. In short, a component of her vital systems has been rewritten. Only a very small percentage of annihilation factors possess such powerful poisons... And Headmistress Fuyajoh fought alongside you two hundred years ago against the mythic-grade Leviathan, Lady Saika... For it to be activating now must mean that it was inflicted then."

"...Dear me, this won't do," Ao responded. "You have a sharp attendant there, Saika."

"...I wondered why a mage of your caliber would use such an inefficient ritual as that *nuptial ceremony*...," Kuroe said. "But now it all makes sense."

Confused, Ruri raised a hand into the air. "H-hold on a sec, Kuroe. Can't you explain?"

Her response was only natural.

"The curse inscribed into Headmistress Fuyajoh is extremely potent," Kuroe continued with a nod. "It eats away at its target's body day by day, until eventually they die. That process would probably take several years for a regular human, maybe twenty for a mage—thirty at most."

"...What...?" Ruri's eyes bulged.

"...This is embarrassing," Ao muttered with a self-deprecating sigh. "Two hundred years ago, when I fought the Leviathan with Saika, I took home a little souvenir... But I couldn't afford to die. As a mage, I had become an indispensable part in protecting this world. You understand what I mean, don't you, Saika? If I were to die, what would become of all this? Don't tell me you haven't asked yourself that question?"

"..."

Mushiki's voice caught in his throat.

"So you created clones of yourself and transferred your soul from body to body to resist the ever-approaching specter of death...," Kuroe continued softly. "But since the cloning process only creates identical copies of the mage Ao Fuyajoh, they, too, are equally short-lived. Even if your soul is transferred while the body is still in its teenage years, you would still need a replacement roughly every decade."

"Huh...?" With a sullen face, Ruri tightened her hand around her chest.

She must have been heartbroken by the surprising news that she had only a limited life expectancy, and by Ao's tragic decision.

Perhaps having noticed this, Ao narrowed her eyes. "...I know my sins. I won't make excuses for myself. Someday, I'm sure, I'll receive just punishment."

"What are you saying, Lady Ao?! You didn't act out of selfishness," Asagi protested.

"...I see...," Kuroe said with a faint sigh.

Her expression was tinged with sympathy and understanding, along with unspoken admonishment for a dear friend's descent into immorality. "Headmistress Fuyajoh. I respect your dedication to and love for this world. But..." She paused, her eyes narrowing as though to hold back her sorrow. "But why didn't you trust those you love more?"

"Huh...?"

"—."

Ao let out a stunned gasp—while Mushiki caught his breath.

During the battle earlier, Kuroe had mentioned just how similar she and Ao really were.

And what she had said a moment ago was certainly true. Ao's decision to sacrifice many for the sake of one was indeed unforgivable.

But there was one clear difference between the actions of the two women.

Mushiki was living proof of that.

"...I understand all too well the love you have for the world, for those who live and breathe on this planet. If I was in the same situation as you, perhaps I would have had similar thoughts," Mushiki said, following Kuroe's lead.

He had no idea if he was qualified to say all this, to speak on Saika's behalf.

However, right now he *was* Saika Kuozaki. And he was one hundred percent sure that she would have said just this, being in much the same situation as Ao herself.

"But let me ask you... Is Ruri—are Asagi and the other students of the Ark—are they all so weak that they can only survive with your protection? Is there no one who can follow in your footsteps, no mage capable of matching, or dare I say it, surpassing your achievements?"

"Th-that's..."

I'm entrusting you with my world, Saika had said on their first meeting.

If she hadn't done what she had, both of them would have died and the entire world would have collapsed.

In a way, this was perhaps little more than wisdom gained after the event.

But even so...Saika had trusted him, and *en*trusted him, with everything.

She had believed in him, as weak and as inadequate as he was.

And that was precisely why he was still alive today.

"Even if we can use magic to prolong our lives, that doesn't mean we should live forever. Eventually, the time must come for us to hand the torch to the next generation."

He could feel the corners of his eyes growing warm. His emotions were perhaps running a little high, given that he was speaking now as Saika—but he continued all the same, without pausing to wipe away his tears. "So we can't—we mustn't—rob our successors of that opportunity... We bear that responsibility to the future."

"…I—I…" Ao choked up, covering her face with her hands.

If she had prolonged her life merely for her own sake, those words would have been without meaning.

But Ao, like Saika, was simply a mage who loved the world above all else, who sought to protect it from harm.

And that was why Mushiki had to speak up now.

At last, Ao lifted her face, her eyes reddened from crying. "…You're right. You're exactly right… I've always known it, somewhere deep inside. This warped state of affairs can't go on forever… I was scared. Like a parent unable to let go of their child. Always worrying if these children can really survive without me."

"Lady Ao…," Asagi said with a pained look, drawing close to her.

Ao rested a hand on the Azure's, then turned her gaze toward Ruri. "…Ruri," she called out.

"Yes…," she answered nervously.

"…You may think this apology a little too late, but I'm sorry," she said with a look as though freed from her inner demons. "I almost robbed you—robbed the world—of your future."

"…"

Ruri remained silent for a long moment, before giving a loud snort. "It's a bit late for that. Seriously, you think people's bodies are yours to do whatever you want with?" She paused. "…It's true you've been protecting the oceans for countless years. But don't deny the achievements of all the different versions of *you* who made it possible."

"Ruri…," Ao began—but she was interrupted before she could continue.

The reason was simple—the Ark had just been hit by the strongest tremor yet.

"Gah…"

"Is that…?"

"Ngh…!"

Ao was able to remain on her feet, thanks to the Azures' help, but she let out a violent cough before turning to Mushiki and the others. "…If the Leviathan really is back, the world will be sent to the depths of the sea. That's no idle joke… I know I've made a mess of things here, but I wonder if you'll still lend me a hand. I'll need your help to defeat that vile creature," she said, flashing them a bloodstained smile.

She certainly was asking a lot there. After all, she had only just tried to usurp Ruri's body, and until just a few minutes ago, they had been caught up in the heat of battle.

But even so, Mushiki nodded without the slightest hesitation.

Because he was sure that would be how Saika would respond.

"Of course. Defending the world is our calling."

In the raging depths of a jet-black sea, several strange silhouettes had begun to rise.

One by one, they might have been mistaken for huge arches—semicircular *somethings* rising from the water's rippling surface.

The problem was their number and scale.

It wasn't long before those shapes—too numerous to guess their exact number—filled the horizon. A spectacle that one might easily have mistaken for a prank or some piece of avant-garde art, was now spreading along Japan's Pacific coast.

Those who were lucky enough—or rather, *un*lucky enough—to witness it for themselves could never have guessed it, but those arches were all connected deep below the water.

"."

The mythic-grade annihilation factor the Leviathan twisted its oversized body as its deafening shriek filled the cloud-covered sky.

"—."

A tense silence fell over Hollow Ark's operations center.

The reason really was quite simple—up on the main monitor wall was projected an image of the Leviathan, a mythic-grade annihilation factor.

Its impossibly long body lay there in the ocean as far as the eye could see. It was so ridiculously large that it made the krakens they had encountered the other day look like small fry. The sheer unreality of it all reminded Mushiki of noodles left to soak in broth.

"...Dear, dear me..."

The one who broke the tense silence was one of the only other mages here who had seen this creature once before—Ao.

"Look how shabby you've become," she scoffed, her lips twisted into a sneer.

For a moment, Mushiki thought those words were meant to alleviate the chilling fear that had filled everyone present—but he was wrong.

Ao's expression betrayed nothing of the sort. Indeed, on closer inspection, the Leviathan's body up on the monitor was almost completely devoid of flesh; its warped bones were exposed to the air.

It was like a skeletal specimen in a museum, or a fish that had been haphazardly eaten and discarded. Its huge size was certainly overwhelming, but like Ao had said, it was nothing if not wretchedly threadbare.

"Lady Saika," Kuroe said.

"...Ah."

Yet its zombielike appearance reminded Mushiki of something else again.

"It looks like the work of Clara's fourth substantiation," he replied brusquely.

"Hmm..." There was a twitch to Ao's eye. "I wouldn't have expected to hear that name here. The Leviathan's resurrection... I was wondering how on earth it had come back. You're saying the Ouroboros did this?"

"Probably...," Mushiki answered. "Clara Tokishima's fourth substantiation, Reincarfect, has the power to revive people where they died. It stands to reason that it might work on a Mythologia defeated ages past."

A faint murmur spread throughout the operations center.

But that couldn't be helped. After all, this raised the prospect of other mythic-grade annihilation factors outside the Leviathan being resurrected, too.

And while they were about to enter battle against the colossal creature, it wouldn't do to send everyone into a panic. So Mushiki raised his voice a little and gave an exaggerated shrug. "Clara can be a bit of a pain. It looks like she wants me to give her another beating."

He heard someone snort somewhere in the room—and with that, the atmosphere began to soften. Saika's presence could have just that kind of effect.

"Either way, we can't just leave it be… What's the situation aboveground?" Ao asked.

"…*I can fill you in on that one,*" echoed a familiar voice in response.

The next moment, a new window opened on the monitor, with Erulka addressing them over videochat.

Right. In order to coordinate with forces aboveground, Mushiki had asked Hildegarde to establish a direct connection to the Garden.

"Oh? It's been a long time, Erulka. I'm glad to see you looking well."

"*It's been ages, Ao. You don't look particularly sprightly there. Knocking on death's door, one might say.*"

The Azures looked on nervously at this greeting, but Ao covered her mouth with her fan and let out an amused laugh. "You'll hold your tongue for nothing, I see."

"*Everything's a mess up here. In all likelihood, there's no way to avoid being submerged. The world will be swallowed by the sea, just as it was two hundred years ago… The Garden and the other schools have set up barriers to prepare for the tsunami. All we can do now is pray that you defeat the Leviathan during the window for reversible annihilation.*"

As it implied, *annihilation factor* was a generic term for beings capable of destroying the world. Their emergence, whenever it happened, inevitably left some degree of devastation in their wake.

But at the same time, whenever such an entity reared its head, the world *system* saved a record of its current state. If the annihilation factor could be defeated during the window for reversible annihilation, the damage sustained would, for all intents and purposes, never have taken place.

For that reason, no matter how powerful their opponent, the task that now fell to Mushiki and the others was clear.

They had to defeat the Leviathan during the window for reversible annihilation, no matter what.

If, for whatever reason, they proved unable to do so, the world's fate would be forever recorded as having sunk to the bottom of the ocean.

"Leave it to me. So long as I'm standing, I won't let it have its way with our world," Mushiki declared in response to Erulka's warning.

"*Ooh...*" An excited murmur spread throughout the operations center.

Ao, however, gave an amused shrug. "...Oh-ho, how noble of you. But we do have something to be grateful for. As luck would have it, you're still in great shape, Saika... While not at its full strength, we're facing a Mythologia. No matter how many mages we have, no half-hearted counterattack can hope to be effective... Of those currently here, who might stand a chance against that monster—yes, there are only two."

Mushiki tilted his head in consternation. It wasn't that he didn't understand what Ao was saying—he did—but he just didn't see the point of saying it aloud.

"You and me, you mean?" he asked.

The Azures, and Ruri, too, all nodded. Naturally. Saika and Ao's victory over the Leviathan at its full strength two hundred years ago was the stuff of legend.

However, there were two among them who didn't agree with that assessment—Kuroe and Ao. Kuroe lowered her gaze in silence, while Ao broke into a soft chuckle.

"Enough with the jokes," she said. "Or were you just being considerate? If I could wield my full strength, perhaps. But in this body, on the cusp of death, I would be no more than a liability."

Hearing this, Mushiki's eyes widened in shock. But she had a good point. After all, that was precisely why she had been so intent on moving to a new body. In fact, there was a very real possibility that his last remark might have been taken as a quip made in bad humor.

But in that case, the other possible fighter—

"It's you, Ruri," Ao said, closing her eyes and gesturing to her with her folding fan.

"...M-me?" she repeated in surprise, pointing to her own face.

"Yes. You, I'm quite sure, should be able to eliminate our enemy... Can I leave this task in your hands?"

"—." Ruri stared back wide-eyed in astonishment at this request. "...Yes. I'll do my best." She bowed after a short pause.

"Very good." Ao nodded in satisfaction. "Now, everyone, take your places... Notify all students—the school will now shift to type-one battle deployment... Our target is the Mythologia, the Leviathan. Let's deal it a crushing blow... Hollow Ark, move out."

"This is a notice to all students. The school will now shift to type-one battle deployment. For your own safety, please take your designated positions... I repeat. The school will now shift to type-one battle deployment. For your own safety—"

Throughout the Ark, a shrill broadcast echoed.

In response, the students who still remained outside on the grounds hurried to the underground evacuation shelters.

It wasn't long before the school was left utterly deserted.

Once this was complete, the underwater city began to *change*.

The shops and lamps that lined the streets retreated into the ground, protected behind solid walls. Next, the earth split open, reconfiguring itself with a loud motorized sound.

Soon, the townscape was transformed into a fortresslike structure, with the central school building serving as its main keep.

"Impressive," Mushiki whispered as he watched all this unfold.

"Yes... I had heard rumors about Hollow Ark's assault submarine configuration, but this is my first time actually seeing it for myself," Ruri said, overcome by deep emotion.

Judging by her voice, she seemed slightly nervous, agitated even. Mushiki glanced at her, flashing her a comforting smile. "Are you scared?"

"...A little," she answered, making no effort to hide her feelings. "...It wasn't like I could refuse, but I'd be lying if I said I'm confident about facing that thing." Her hands were slightly trembling.

But that was perfectly reasonable. She wasn't just facing a mythic-class annihilation factor. To Ao, the word *entrust* carried a much deeper meaning.

"You can do it," Mushiki encouraged her.

"Right... I suppose...," Ruri responded nervously. "There's one other thing..."

"Go on?"

"I'm still not sure whether I'm talking to Madam Witch or Mushiki."

"..."

At this, Mushiki broke out into a nervous sweat.

...Well, from her perspective, that was only natural. A lot had happened between learning the truth about Ao and the appearance of the Leviathan, but it wasn't like she could possibly forget.

"Since when? When exactly? I feel like I've told you a whole lot about Mushiki, Madam Witch..."

"...Ah, you're right. I'll explain everything once this is all over."

"Very well. But can I ask one thing?"

"What?"

"That when you do, it's as Madam Witch."

"Oh? And why is that?"

"So long as you're Madam Witch, I think I'll be able to maintain at least a *little* self-control."

"...I'll do my best," Mushiki said, fighting to keep his voice from shaking.

This might have all sounded like light banter to anyone listening in, but looking at Ruri's unfocused gaze and her trembling fingertips, she seemed to be trying to keep herself in check: *Please...don't let me become a murderer...*

But the next moment—

"You both look ready," a voice said from behind them.

Both Mushiki and Ruri turned around to find Kuroe approaching.

"Kuroe…?"

"…H-hold on, what are *you* doing here?!" Ruri cried out in alarm.

But that was to be expected. After all, the Ark was about to set out, and all personnel other than Mushiki and Ruri were supposed to have moved to the underground evacuation shelters.

But Kuroe paid her no heed. "I have a suggestion to make," she said calmly.

"A suggestion …?"

"Yes. It mustn't be you who defeats the Leviathan, Lady Saika."

"…*Huh?*" Mushiki and Ruri were startled, and they exchanged confused looks.

"Type-one battle deployment, engaged!"

"Hollow Ark assault submarine reconfiguration complete!"

"We're ready to launch on your signal!"

While formally called an *operations center*, the Ark's headquarters was quite different from those of other mage-training institutes.

A single seat was set up in the center of the room, with other staff members seated at monitors lined up along its outer edge. All in all, it called to mind the bridge of a battleship.

And so it should. The Ark was a mobile fortress designed to circumnavigate the ocean, and this operations center functioned as both a command center and a bridge.

"Good. The Ark will now head out to defeat the mythic-class Leviathan," Ao uttered, leaning to one side on the command chair.

Every breath brought immense pain to her lungs, and if she wasn't careful, she could have another coughing fit. Yet somehow, she managed to keep it all down… After all, if the captain of the ship started vomiting up blood while directing operations against the Leviathan, morale would be sure to plummet.

"Are you ready? Saika? Ruri?" she asked, looking up at the main monitor.

"Ah... Yes," sounded Saika's voice over the communications channel.

"We're all right...I think...," Ruri added.

"...?"

Something about her voice suggested barely contained panic. Ao tilted her head in concern. "What's the matter? Is there a problem?"

"No... No problems. This isn't beyond Saika Kuozaki's abilities."

"R-right. I'm sure we'll be fine."

"Why does it sound like you're giving each other a pep talk...?"

"Not at all."

"No way, no way."

"..."

Ao would have been lying if she said she wasn't concerned by those responses, but she could hardly let on to the command crew. And so, taking a deep breath to collect herself, she issued a fresh command: "Then let's roll out. Hollow Ark—surface!"

"Roger that!" the crew responded in unison.

Stronger than when the krakens had attacked—

More violent than when the Leviathan had first appeared—

The Ark *shook*.

But that was only natural.

After all, it wasn't being shaken from the outside now, but from within as it roved across the bottom of the seafloor.

Yet Mushiki and Ruri, in the midst of those incredible tremors, had their minds on something else entirely.

"...Um, Madam Witch? I'm still not quite sure what's going on."

"Mm-hmm."

"...Kuroe, did you really mean that...?" Ruri asked, visibly nervous.

"Right." Mushiki stepped in, doing his best to keep his own anxiety under wraps. "But if it *is* possible, it's our only real option."

"...But, Madam Witch..." Ruri hesitated, biting her lip.

At that moment, a storm of sand rose from where the Ark had been situated, covering the area in a mist-like haze.

Then, tearing through the dust cloud—

The Ark rose straight for the water's surface.

"...!"

The thick dome of air rose higher in altitude, avoiding or pushing away schools of fish, drifting debris, and the massive body of the Leviathan as it thrashed about.

At last, the Ark reached the surface.

But the sight beyond the dome was far from elegant.

Whether owing to the appearance of the annihilation factor or mere coincidence, black clouds plunged the sky at sunset into deep darkness, and all the while, violent storms were brewing. A tempest raged at sea, and every time the Leviathan moved its long body, the water surged, transforming the surrounding area into a hellish waterscape.

Although the Ark was huge, it was no more than a leaf floating in the endless expanse of the ocean. No sooner had it risen to the surface than further tremors reached Mushiki and the others.

But he had no time to accustom himself to the shaking, nor even to prepare himself, for the very next moment, Ao's voice sounded in his earpiece: *"Your opponent is the Leviathan. It's repulsively huge, but don't let that stop you... Aim for the head. Send it flying. And don't let it shake you off."*

Without waiting for a response, the outer edge of the Ark was bathed in a magical glow—and the vessel set off. Now, a different kind of tremor plagued them, along with a nameless sense of pressure.

The Ark ploughed forward at full speed, its huge hull tearing through the raging sea.

Yet—

"_____!"

The next moment, a roar like distant thunder shook the air.

"That sound—"

"It's the Leviathan... Maybe it noticed us?" Ruri interrupted with a frown.

Then, as if to prove her right, the space in front of the Ark warped, and several *spheres* formed in midair.

Those *spheres* rippled along the water's surface, stirring up potent whirlpools before firing jets of water like rays of blinding light directly at the Ark.

"Gah...!"

With a brilliant flash, the water hit the barrier of air around the Ark before being swallowed by the ocean—sending a shockwave hitting Mushiki and the others like a bomb exploding at close range.

But it didn't end there. Countless more *spheres* started launching jets of water all at once.

They were too many to count, all of them being fired with the intent to kill.

The Ark sped forward to avoid them, seemingly without regard for those riding inside—but eventually it, too, reached its limit.

Just as more *spheres* appeared ahead of them, there was a brilliant flash.

"What...?!"

The initial shockwave had triggered violent tremors and exploded into the walls of the Ark. So Mushiki's body stiffened in preparation for the coming impact.

But even after a few moments, the expected blast failed to hit.

The flash of light that he had assumed would shatter the keep was instead repelled by the shining dome of air, recoiling backward.

"They deflected it...!" Mushiki wheezed.

The next moment, Ao's voice sounded once more from his earpiece: *"When the Leviathan threatens us, we'll have the students erect a magic barrier. That being said, it's a mythic-grade beast, that thing..."*

"Ah..."

"...We'll only be able to deflect it one more time."

"...That's cutting it a bit fine, don't you think?" Mushiki responded.

"I don't need you to tell us that," Ao retorted, annoyed. *"I know just*

how formidable it is… But it ought to be enough," she added, her voice carrying a hint of a smile.

Before Mushiki knew otherwise, a fresh object appeared in front of the Ark.

A long, bony body, twisting through the sea. There was no end in sight, yet its tip rose into the air like a menacing sickle.

"—."

The creature's skull was composed of bone and the barest fragments of skin and flesh, and possessed a serpentine, dragon-like, conical shape. Devoid of expression, its imposing mien portended approaching disaster.

Its most distinctive feature, however, was its forehead.

From the forehead of that dragon-shaped skull protruded what looked like the upper half of a human body. Well, if you could call the hulking multiarmed silhouette *human*, that is.

"That's—"

"The Leviathan's head."

"—————————————————————!"

As if responding to Mushiki and Ruri, the Leviathan let out a fiendish howl from its two mouths.

Though it wasn't clear which organs were producing the sound, it was loud enough to be heard miles away, causing the air itself to pulsate painfully around them.

The creature turned its huge, cavernous eyes toward them, its dragon's maw opening wide.

Then, a huge *sphere* of water, larger by several orders of magnitude compared to the previous ones, began to swirl in its mouth.

Its effect would be every bit as large and powerful as the previous strikes. If they sustained a direct hit, they would be crushed in seconds.

Yet—

"*Repeating the exact same old tricks it played two hundred years ago…!*"

Ao's voice sounded over their earpieces—and the next moment, the Ark was covered with an unprecedentedly dense barrier of magical energy.

"…!"

It leaped from the surface of the water high into the air, descending upon the monster as if to sate its hunger.

With a tremendous shock and a deafening roar, the *sphere* forming in its mouth burst open.

No matter how gargantuan the Leviathan's mouth was, it couldn't possibly swallow the entire Ark. And indeed, its lower jaw bones were soon crushed, unable to endure the weight of the floating city.

"*Saika! Ruri! Now's your chance! Show it what you've got!*" Ao cried out amid the fierce aftershocks.

"Let's go, Ruri."

"R-right…!"

With that, the two of them kicked off from the roof and took to the sky.

Three-stage world crests appeared over both of their heads, their second and third substantiations manifesting in their hands and around their bodies.

Mushiki practically glided through the sky—and as soon as he reached the Leviathan's head, he raised his second substantiation staff high above him.

"Stellarium!"

The next moment, the staff blazed with a resplendence of color.

In response, the raging ocean below and the black clouds overhead began to pulsate with a thunderous beat.

Water, fog, thunder—the elements moved in accordance with Mushiki's will, binding, carving, and piercing the Leviathan's large body.

It was as if the entire landscape had lent him its power—leaving his foe to writhe and howl in agony.

But even though not in perfect condition, the creature was still a Mythologia. And if it was Clara who had resurrected it, it would no doubt regenerate in no time at all. At best, Mushiki would probably be able to stop its movements for only a few seconds.

But that was fine. In fact, that was exactly what he wanted.

After all—Mushiki wasn't trying to defeat the Leviathan here.

"Hah…!"

Once again, he raised his staff and activated Stellarium, manipulating the seawater to become a huge veil—completely enshrouding his own figure.

"Status?!" Ao barked in the operations center.

The command crew responded at once:

"Wall integrity is at thirty percent! Preparing to withdraw!"

"Headmistress Kuozaki and Lady Ruri have activated their second and third substantiations!"

"The headmistress—she's restrained the Leviathan!"

Ao clenched her fists as the reports came in.

The main monitor was now displaying the Ark's forward trajectory—and ahead, the Leviathan was now contained within Saika's Stellarium.

So far, so good. All that remained was for Saika and Ruri to finish it off.

"…Huh?"

Yet Ao's eyes widened in alarm as she watched the video feed on the main monitor.

But that was only natural. After all, Saika's veil of water seemed to have completely vanished.

"…!"

There, in its place, was Mushiki Kuga.

Feeling like someone had played a cheap parlor trick on her, she wheezed, "What…?! What's Mushiki doing out there?!"

"—."

Having reverted to his original form within the veil of water, Mushiki let gravity do the rest.

Since he was no longer in Saika's body, her techniques were now beyond him. Not just her third substantiation, but even her basic flight magic, too. The result was inevitable.

But this was what the situation demanded of him.

Holding fast to his consciousness, he thought back to Kuroe's suggestion earlier...

"Simply put, our strategy is to approach the Leviathan, flank it from opposing sides, and then destroy it."

"Right. You're not trying to say that won't be enough or anything, are you?"

"No. Of course, with this being an aquatic battle, I can't make any guarantees, but I'm quite certain that the two of you ought to be able to defeat this present incarnation... But it won't be enough just to defeat it."

"...? What are you saying? Is there a problem?" Ruri asked, visibly confused.

"The world will indeed be saved as long as you defeat it. And the water will subside as well," Kuroe continued. "But the effects on mages who have witnessed this annihilation factor won't be undone even if you defeat it... Ao's body, poisoned by its curse, will soon reach its limit. And you, too, Ruri—with Ao's blood running through your veins, you can only expect to live another decade or so."

"But that's...," Ruri stammered, falling silent.

She couldn't possibly have forgotten, but no one would be able to stay calm after being so brusquely reminded of that fact.

Yet Mushiki sensed some hidden meaning behind Kuroe's words—a possibility.

"...Are you saying there's a way to deal with the poison?"

Right. Kuroe had said it herself—she had a suggestion.

"It would involve considerable risk, but yes, there is a chance—a slight one, I should point out," she said, narrowing her eyes. "Though we might call it a *poison*, the Leviathan's toxin is more like a magic formula than an actual substance or compound. Which is precisely why there is no antidote. The only way to break the spell is to have the caster release it. Remember, the spell persisted even after the Leviathan's death two hundred years ago. Even today, Ao and her descendants continue to suffer." Her voice was as calm as ever, but her passion rang out all the same. "We can't say for sure why Clara Tokishima resurrected the Leviathan, but this presents us with a once-in-a-lifetime opportunity—the possibility of extinguishing an eternal poison for which all hope was lost."

Ruri leaned forward, tempted by Kuroe's proposal. "B-but how exactly *do* we get it to undo the curse?"

As if she had been waiting for this very question, Kuroe looked at Mushiki. "Have you forgotten, Ruri? You've seen it for yourself—the power to erase substantiations."

Right. Mushiki's second substantiation, his translucent sword.

The true nature of the technique remained unknown, but one thing was certain—it was capable of erasing an opposing substantiation.

Mushiki stared at his feet, concentrating as hard as he could.

He had been a mage for only a short time. Though he had been exposed to various aspects of magic while in Saika's body, he wasn't at a level where he could freely use his own powers.

For him to manifest his second substantiation, he would need strong—incredibly strong—emotions.

For example, thoughts of Saika. When he thought of her, his chest panged, and an uncontrollable wellspring of emotions surged in his heart. That was essential in the production of magic.

"..."

But—

This time, there was someone else in his thoughts—Ruri.

No matter the cost, he would save her from her fated death.

That thought burned deep in his heart, intensely, brilliantly.

"Second Substantiation..."

A two-layered world crest appeared above him—unfurling from both sides like a warped crown.

"Hollow Edge...!" he cried.

A sword of clear glass appeared in his hand.

By then, he was already approaching the Leviathan's head.

"Ruri. I'm here for you."
Gripping the Hollow Edge with both hands—
"Aaarrrggghhh!"
He plunged his blade deep into the Leviathan's forehead.

"…!"
Ruri grimaced at the scorching pain spreading through her chest.
She inserted a finger into the folds of her armor—and let out a small gasp.
The marking, which just a few short moments ago was etched deep into her skin, was now gone, as if it had never existed.
"…Mushiki…!"
She jolted backward as she came to her senses, crouching down to launch herself up into the sky. Mushiki couldn't fly in his current state. At this rate, he would plunge straight into the sea.
But the next moment, a bird of blue flames appeared beneath Mushiki's feet as he fell past the Leviathan's head, holding him in place.
There could be no mistaking it—that was Ao's second substantiation.
As if to confirm what she already knew, Ao's voice sounded in her earpiece: *"…Ruri, what in the world is going on out there?"* Then, clearly perturbed, she added, *"Where did Mushiki just come from? Where did Saika go…? And why is the curse lifted?"*
"…I—I don't know…," Ruri responded with a sigh.
It was true—she had yet to hear Mushiki's and Saika's explanation about the precise nature of their relationship, and she still didn't quite grasp the full picture of Mushiki's second substantiation.
"…But one thing is certain," she began.
"…What?"
"There's no stopping Madam Witch and Mushiki," she said, wiping her tears away as she turned back to the Leviathan.
To be honest, she *was* ill at ease about taking on a mythic-grade annihilation factor, and she would have been lying if she said that the role Ao had given her didn't feel like a burden. Perhaps, even standing now on the frontlines, she still wasn't fully prepared.

Until just a few seconds ago, that is.

Mushiki had so brilliantly fulfilled his role in battle and had been successfully rescued by Ao's second substantiation.

He must have exhausted his magic to break the curse. His transparent sword had already vanished from his hands, as had the world crest glimmering above his head. On top of that, he seemed to be covered all over in wounds.

Despite that special technique of his, he was, after all, still a novice mage. Unable to even wield flight magic without Ao's help, he would no doubt have plummeted straight into the ocean below.

Yet in spite of all that, he had single-handedly attacked the mighty Mythologia.

And it had all been for her. To break the curse that had been placed over the Fuyajoh family.

Ah. The situation might have been different, but here it was—the very scene that Ruri had longed for as a child.

"Ah…," she breathed, releasing an outpouring of emotion.

To be honest, she was still disoriented by the inexplicable phenomenon of Mushiki transforming into Saika, and Saika transforming into Mushiki. She couldn't begin to comprehend the nature of what she had seen.

But deep in her heart, she was relieved that it was them.

Saika had paved the way forward—and Mushiki had guided her down it.

The two individuals she respected most had gone to such extreme lengths for her. She couldn't dawdle here worrying forever.

I'm glad I studied under Saika.

I'm glad Mushiki's my brother.

From here on out, the task was hers.

While its curse had been lifted, the Leviathan itself was still very much alive. Its impossibly long body, resembling nothing if not a skeletal fossil, writhed in agony.

If she failed here, Saika's trust in her, Ao's confidence, and Mushiki's love all would have been for naught. She couldn't stand that thought.

But it was mysterious.

"Ha-ha…"

Her heart now knew no pressure or fear.

There was only the greatest of emotions, the passion that drove her.

Lifting a hand into the air, she drew an insignia with burning, intense emotions.

"…Day for day, night for night."

A three-layered world crest shaped like a demon's head appeared above her—joined next by another fang-like stroke.

"Until eternity and the life to come, there will be no time for darkness to spread."

The naginata in her hands and the armor protecting her body were both bathed in gleaming fire.

As if responding to this change, the ocean floor began to emit a bluish-white glow.

"Now behold! The citadel of eternal night!"

She cried the name of the strongest technique she had:

"Fourth Substantiation: World of Infinite Nightless Days!"

A moment later—a huge fortress appeared, tearing through the raging sea.

"Ah…"

Lying on the back of a bird of flame, Mushiki looked on, dumbfounded, at the scene transpiring before him.

It was a fantastic sight.

A magnificent castle tower, a blue bonfire scattering sparks like petals, emerged out of the darkness. All at once, the dark night was painted over, the thick clouds and the leaden sea replaced by brilliant moonlight.

The Leviathan, thrashing around underwater and letting out wails of agony, was exposed to the void, being pushed upward by the rising fortress.

"Ruri…!" Mushiki called out.

The reason was simple. Around her in every direction, countless *spheres* of water had appeared.

If they fired at her all at once, it would be well-nigh impossible for her to shoot them all down.

Yet—

"…It's okay." Ruri, bathed in divine light, gave a carefree smile.

"—."

Amid the light, Ruri was filled with a sense of omnipotence.

Her fourth substantiation—the strongest level and the ultimate goal of any modern-day mage.

Certainly, there was a great deal of risk involved when pushing oneself this far. It wasn't something that could just be used whenever the fancy struck.

But once manifested—

"No one can defeat me! Not except for Madam Witch!" she shouted to the heavens, wielding the new power that flowed through her body.

At that moment, the Leviathan's *spheres* erupted into balls of light.

They must have numbered at least a couple of hundred, and she couldn't possibly hope to eradicate them all just with her Luminous Blade.

But she didn't need weapons now.

With a blinding flash, the jets of water struck her from all sides.

But—

"Hmm…"

Her lips twisted into a sneer as she accepted the bombardment head on.

Though her entire body was pierced by barrages of cutting water, and even though a single *sphere* ought to have been fatal, she was completely unharmed.

And that was as it should be—all thanks to her fourth substantiation.

Having activated it, she could freely fix the state of anything and everything within range at will.

In other words, while using her fourth substantiation, she could maintain her unharmed state no matter what kind of attack was dealt to her.

And *fixing a state* didn't end there.

"Aaarrrggghhh!"

Launching herself into the sky, she slashed at the Leviathan with her Luminous Blade.

In an instant, the tapering sword of blue light sliced off the titan's arms, the Leviathan's wails echoing all around.

The Leviathan had been resurrected with Clara's powers—and if Ruri's experiences in their previous encounter under the Garden's library were anything to go by, its body would continue to regenerate so long as Clara didn't lift the spell.

But now that she had *assured* the severed state of the Leviathan's limbs, they plunged silently into the sea without regenerating.

And that wasn't all.

Blue flames spread along the creature's shoulder where her blade had hit it, and sparks of fire shot down its long body.

Under regular circumstances, those flames would abate within moments.

But Ruri had made it so that they would never go out, and so now they enveloped the creature's body.

Of course, this state would continue only for as long as her magical energy lasted and her fourth substantiation was in effect.

But the Leviathan itself seemed to have been only partially resurrected within Clara's fourth substantiation.

"Let's see which of us can last the longest, you evil cow."

Ruri stared down at the burning Leviathan with a ferocious grin, bathed in the light of the flames ripping through it.

"!"

At last, the Leviathan let out a final death wail as it crashed sideward into the sea.

Even underwater, the flames from her attack continued to burn until finally the giant creature's carcass was completely consumed.

"...Did you see that, moron?"

Having watched until the end, Ruri deactivated her abilities and fell from the sky.

She felt as if a gentle hand had reached out and caught her before she could crash into the waters below—but having already exhausted her magical energy, she wasn't entirely sure who it belonged to.

Chapter 6
Here and Now, After
⇥ Years of Unspoken Feelings ⇤

Ruri had always loved her brother.

Perhaps that was because he was always kind to her, or maybe because he considered her adorable. Whenever they went shopping together, he would offer to carry the heavy bags, and he would always give her the biggest piece of candy.

To Ruri, he was a gentle older brother, someone who had been by her side for as long as she could remember, always looking out for her.

And she loved him for it.

That was when she realized—she couldn't imagine a world without him.

But if there had ever been a single defining moment—

Yes, it could only be that time seven years ago.

She remembered his back.

Small, but to her, it was large as he stepped forward to protect her.

"...Mushiki...?" Ruri called out, stunned by what she had seen.

For a moment, the figure before her hadn't been that of her familiar brother.

The reason was simple—a crown-like mass of light now hovered above the young Mushiki's head.

* * *

Ruri and Mushiki were born into a family of magicians called the Fuyajoh, but to be perfectly honest, neither had trained particularly diligently during their childhood.

This was because their mother was opposed to the rest of the family's stance. As such, they had resided in the so-called *outside world* away from the Ark, where their relatives lived. Their lives were almost the same as those of regular people.

They went to a normal elementary school, played with normal friends, and ate normal meals—and while they did on the rare occasion have one or two strange guests, and they did occasionally make their way to some strange locale for one event or another, as far as Ruri and Mushiki were concerned, such trips were like nothing more than the normal practice of returning to one's hometown for the Bon festival and New Year's.

That day, however, Ruri's world changed completely.

An annihilation factor had appeared near where the family lived.

Annihilation factor—a catch-all term for entities capable of destroying the world.

If such events could be overcome during the window for reversible annihilation, their effects wouldn't be recorded in the world's history.

As such, the destruction, the loss of their family home, the ruined landscape—all should have been returned to normal once a mage defeated the rampaging enemy.

But although Ruri was lacking in skills, she was still a mage.

Her wounds wouldn't have returned to normal, and any lost limbs wouldn't have grown back.

If she had died, her life would have been irrevocably lost.

Yet—

"...Are you hurt, Ruri?"

The figure looking over his shoulder as he asked this was none other than her brother, Mushiki.

Yes. His gentle smile was the same as ever. It was hard to imagine that just now, he had manifested a substantiation of his own and defeated the annihilation factor.

"…! Mushiki! Mushiki!" She wept, tears streaming down her cheeks.

Mushiki flashed her a quiet smile, gently stroking the back of her head. "Don't worry. I'll protect you, Ruri."

His pleasant touch helped ease the chill that had locked her in place, a sense of relief flowing through her heart.

But all she could do was repeat her brother's name, her tears never stopping.

There was so much that she wanted to say.

So many feelings that she wanted to share with him.

But the young Ruri didn't know how to put them into words.

Now, she finally understood.

Ah—this was what she had felt back then.

Ruri had fallen in love with him, her heart—

"…!"

She woke with a start—jolting upright and glancing around.

She was in a large Japanese-style room, in a comfortable futon laid out on high-quality tatami floor.

There could be no mistaking it—this was the room she had been assigned to after moving to the Ark.

"Huh…? What am I…? What happened…?" she murmured as she rubbed her eyes.

Her body felt heavy—exhausted as if she had just finished a long sprint up a mountain road before nodding off to sleep.

As she became more awake, her memories began to return to her.

Right. She had gone to see Lady Ao to voice her complaints but had instead been placed under house arrest until Saika and the others arrived to rescue her. After that, she had been taken to the main residence, where Ao had knocked her unconscious. The next time she came to, she was—

"…Ah."

The last missing memory fell into place with a click.

"Aaarrrggghhh?!"

Recalling everything that had happened, she jumped up onto her feet.

The soft susurrus of several pinwheels spinning sounded all around.

Even inside the Ark, surrounded by its huge wall of air, the wind was blowing. Apparently, there were artificial air currents within the dome of the underwater city to keep the air from getting stagnant.

"Is this…?"

Mushiki glanced around. There was a cemetery behind the main Fuyajoh residence, with tombstones in orderly lines. Each of them was decorated with fresh flowers, the paths running between them clean and well maintained.

"It isn't an entirely accurate description, but these are essentially the graves of former family heads… For two hundred years, the Leviathan's curse has invaded my life. This is where I mourn the corpses of previous Ao Fuyajohs after choosing my successor," Ao explained, making her way down the gravel path with Asagi by her side.

"Apologies for keeping you waiting… I had to report the news to my children first."

"Not at all. Don't worry about us," Mushiki said.

Ao responded with a weak smile, looked quietly down at the nearest grave, and remained that way in silent prayer.

After a long moment, she slowly raised her face, glancing around with a smile.

"…Perhaps you think me a fool? Or do you scorn me as a hypocrite?" she asked.

"What…? No, nothing like that." Mushiki shook his head.

His words weren't meant as hollow courtesy—he was speaking from the heart. While his opinion on Ao's use of clones to transfer her soul from body to body was much the same as Saika's, it was also true that her actions and attitude spoke of genuine compassion and a wish to atone.

Looking off into the distance, Ao exhaled deeply. "First, allow me to apologize, and to thank you. You did well, stopping the Leviathan."

"It was Ruri who defeated it, not me."

"But you were the one who broke the curse, weren't you?" she asked, reaching up to her chest.

After the battle, she had changed into a fresh set of clothes, and nothing remained of the scar or her spilled blood.

"...When I last saw you, you were but a child. To think how much you've grown... If you're enrolled at the Garden, I suppose Saika has undone the blocks on your memory? But I'm surprised Ruri approved of you becoming a mage."

"Memory blocks...?" Mushiki repeated uncertainly.

For a moment, Ao was startled, then gave a soft shrug. "Surely they can't still be in place? Then how in the world did you become a mage?"

"Well, a whole lot happened..."

He couldn't explain it in detail, so he did his best to brush the question aside.

"If you don't want to discuss it, I won't pry... But that would mean Ruri..."

"...Hasn't acknowledged me yet."

"Hmm... Hah. Ha-ha-ha..." Ao broke into a soft chuckle. "Yes, I can imagine. I wondered how she could have such a huge change of heart for her dear big brother."

"U-um..."

But Ao waved Mushiki's confusion aside. "Ah, apologies. I let myself get carried away... If you want them back, just ask Saika to release the blocks on your memory engrams... You know, Ruri might not like it, but the situation is really quite different compared to last time. I don't know what this Clara Tokishima plans to use the Ouroboros for, but if she can revive fallen Mythologia, then there really is no limit to the strength she can muster." She paused, blinking as if in sudden remembrance. "Speaking of which, where *is* Saika? I haven't seen her since the middle of the battle."

"...Er, well..."

"Don't worry. She's not too far from here, watching over us all," Kuroe answered calmly, approaching to stand beside him.

It was a rather misleading statement, but not quite a lie.

"That's not a promising omen." Ao laughed. "Ah, yes. About Ruri—"

But at that moment—

"Mushikiiiiiiiii! Kuroeeeeeeeee!"

Speak of the devil. Just like that, Ruri came sprinting toward them at incredible speed, kicking up a cloud of dust in her wake—before wrapping her arms around Mushiki's and Kuroe's necks in a strangling embrace.

"I was looking all over for yooouuu…!" she cried, tears pouring from her eyes.

Mushiki broke out into a cold sweat at the sheer ferocity of her hug. "R-Ruri…? Good morning. I'm glad to see you're awake."

"Huh? Ah, yeah. Morning… So, there was something you wanted to tell me, right?"

"…About how you did great in the fight against the Leviathan?"

"N-not that."

"…That you look beautiful today?"

"Not that, either!" she shouted, her cheeks turning red as she tightened the hold around his neck.

He was starting to have difficulty breathing.

"You're full of life for someone who just got out of bed." Ao chuckled, watching from the side.

Only then did Ruri realize that Ao and Asagi were present, too. Still with her arms wrapped around their necks, she gave Ao a polite bob of the head.

"…! Sorry, Lady Ao! Can I borrow these two?!"

"By all means. I still have unanswered questions, but they can wait for now," Ao said. "By the way…which of you will be Ruri's pick? I wonder."

"…Huh?"

Ruri's eyes bulged in response to this teasing question.

"Oh, you know. I meant between Mushiki and Saika," Ao

continued, turning back to Ruri. "Now that the Leviathan's curse is lifted, there's nothing stopping you from marrying whoever you choose. Even if it was only to call off the nuptial ceremony, you wouldn't bring someone you had no feelings for to see me, would you now…? Oh, don't worry. I'm a very open-minded woman when it comes to such things. Believe me when I say this—I won't criticize any partner you choose, Ruri."

"Wh-wh-wha—"

Ruri's face had already turned bright red.

"…E-excuse us!" she cried, grabbing Mushiki and Kuroe and making a run for it.

Left behind, Ao and Asagi looked on, stunned.

"…The Fuyajoh clan has a turbulent future ahead of it, wouldn't you say?" Ao remarked.

"It would appear so," Asagi responded.

The two laughed weakly.

"Come on, you promised me an explanation!"

Having half abducted Mushiki and Kuroe to take them back to the guest quarters on the top floor of the dormitory building, Ruri positioned herself in front of the door to bar any escape.

"…What are you talking about?"

"…I don't know what you mean."

Both Mushiki and Kuroe looked away.

Ruri, however, grabbed them both by the head and forced them to look at her. "I remember everything, you hear me…? I've got a whole lot of questions, but first thing's first." She paused, staring straight into Mushiki's eyes. "Mushiki, you've somehow *become* Madam Witch, haven't you? What on earth is going on? That wasn't just shape-shifting magic. You actually *became* her."

"A-a trick of the eyes, maybe?"

"You think I would mistake Madam Witch?"

He had to admit, she made a compelling argument there. As to be expected from Ruri Fuyajoh, the (unofficial) master appraiser of all things Saika Kuozaki. Mushiki understood at once that any attempt at deception would prove fruitless.

"..."

He glanced at Kuroe.

She seemed to agree. In other words, it was acceptable to let Ruri in on their secret. After giving it more thought, she finally gave him a short nod.

"...All right. I'll talk," Mushiki answered, making up his mind and looking back at Ruri.

That was when he suddenly remembered something.

"Ah, right. Ruri? You said you wanted to hear it from Saika...didn't you?"

"Ah...yes. If it comes from Madam Witch...I might be able...to better hold myself together..." She seemed to be having difficulty keeping herself in check.

...Mushiki had no death wish, and he was going to have to explain everything anyway. He glanced back at Kuroe to make sure.

"Got it... Kuroe?"

"Very well."

With those words, Kuroe rested her hands on his shoulders and pressed her lips up against his own.

"Wh-wh-whaaaaaaaaat?!" Ruri screamed, forcing herself between the two of them and pulling them apart. "Ugh... What the hell?! What are you doing?!" she demanded in confusion.

"...I need magical energy to start a state transformation..."

"This is a necessary step to change Mushiki into Lady Saika. I assure you this is no different to assisted respiration."

"How am I supposed to believe thaaat?!" Ruri thrashed about, before finally falling still. "H-hey... Right, when Mushiki changed into Madam Witch, he—"

She stopped, the blood rushing to her cheeks.

"...I—I'll do it!"

"Huh?"

Mushiki's eyes almost bulged from their sockets at this unexpected outburst, when Ruri grabbed him fast by the shoulders.

"U-um..."

"Th-this is no different to the first and second times! Just leave it to me!"

Judging by her expression, Ruri herself hardly seemed to know what she was saying anymore. Nonetheless, eyes squeezed shut, she leaned in close to Mushiki's face—and pressed her lips lightly against his.

He had grown used to Kuroe's kiss, so this one from Ruri felt somehow different.

"...H-how was that? Did you change?" she asked, her cheeks burning as she timidly opened her eyes.

She could wait as long as she wanted, but there was no sign of any transformation. A look of bewilderment had begun to take root on her face.

"H-huh...? You're supposed to transform, though?" she asked uncertainly, when Kuroe stepped forward.

"I must have neglected to mention this, but when supplying Mushiki with magical energy, you need to place a certain spell on his lips in advance."

"...Hah?" Ruri stared back open-mouthed. "...So you're saying...?"

"That was just a kiss. Not a supply of magical energy."

"..."

Just when Mushiki thought Ruri's cheeks couldn't turn any redder, she buried her face in his chest, her hands slowly tightening around his neck.

"R-Ruri...?"

He braced himself for the worst. Yet—

"...That other time... And this one, too..." she began in a small voice.

"Huh?" Mushiki was startled.

"...I was never able to say it... Thank you. For saving me back then. For always being so kind to me. I was so happy when you called me cute... I love you, Mushiki."

"Ruri..."

She jolted upright as he said her name. Her face was still tinged pink, and tears were welling up in her eyes, but she looked somehow relieved.

"Sorry, Kuroe! I misspoke just before!"

"You did, did you?"

Ruri spun around, pointing right at her:

"That wasn't just a simple kiss—it was a kiss of love!"

⇥ Afterword ⇤

Long time no see. Koushi Tachibana here.

How did you find the third volume of *King's Proposal: The Lapis Knight*? I hope you enjoyed it. I especially like the title, a pun in Japanese that can mean either "lapis lazuli knight" or "Ruri's knight" because the kanji used for Ruri's name is the same as the gemstone's.

So the series is now at three volumes, with a brilliant number "3" emblazoned on the cover. I honestly didn't expect to get this far, so I can't wait to see what happens in Volume 4 and beyond.

The cover shows Ruri Fuyajoh, whom we've known since the first volume, and she's finally showing off her third substantiation. Her design, fusing both traditional Japanese aesthetics and futuristic tech, is really cool, if you ask me—the result of heated discussions until late at night with my editor. The last time I got so excited over something like this was when we were debating whether or not to inflate Vánargandr's thighs in *Date A Live*. But thanks to all that, I think it turned out splendidly.

Now then, this book is only here thanks to the efforts of many individuals.

To my illustrator, Tsunako—sorry again for introducing so many new characters this time around. You've done an excellent job with them all, especially Hildegarde.

To my cover designer, Kusano—superb. After the vibrant cover for Volume 2, this one is just perfect. And Ruri looks so cool!

To my editor—thank you again for all your help. For some reason, all three Japanese volumes have ended at exactly 336 pages with an afterword lasting two pages, but I assure you, that's entirely coincidental.

To everyone in the editorial department and those involved in publication, distribution, and sales—and to you, holding this book now in your hands—I would like to express my heartfelt thanks.

I look forward to seeing you all again next time around.

August 2022, Koushi Tachibana